HENCH

Hench Western Adventures

Book 1

by

Joseph Parks

A PulpPerchPress (P³) Book

Published by PulpPerchPress (P³)

To get a FREE Hench short story
sign up for the Hench mailing list by going to:

JosephParksAuthor.com

Hench Books

Hench
Blood Hoard
All's Jake
Town of Fear

CHAPTER ONE

There was a loud slap, a chair scraped back with force, and a man bellowing in anger and pain. Hench looked up from his bowl of green chili. Across the saloon, the man in question held Gabriela by her wrist and raised a hand to strike her. She looked fierce as she swung at him but missed.

Hench jumped to his feet, but he couldn't reach them in time, so he grabbed a chair and flung it as hard as he could. It crashed into the ranch hand's legs. The man flipped back hard, smashing his head into the floorboards, pulling Gabriela off balance. She fell on top of him and didn't hesitate to punch him in the face.

However, the ranch hand had two friends with him. They scrambled from their chairs to aid their fallen comrade, who needed the help under the onslaught of Gabriela's fists. Hench rushed toward them, but Rogelio, who was the owner of Walter's Saloon, jumped the bar and got to them first.

Unfortunately, despite his bravery, Rogelio was only a bit over five feet tall. The ranch hands were bigger. But that didn't stop him from getting in front of them, putting out his hands. "Please, sirs, do not touch my wife."

The reply came from the closer man, who snapped his fist out, hitting Rogelio in the face. He sat down hard on the gray rough-hewn floorboards. But the distraction gave Hench time to get from his table to theirs.

He also held out his hands. "Easy now, boys."

At half his age, they looked like kids. He was in his forties and they couldn't have been much over twenty. Hench had graying dark brown hair hanging almost to his shoulders and a beard and mustache that had lost the battle and were mostly gray. The ranch hands were also a little bigger than Hench who, in his boots, was five-nine.

The same man who had downed Rogelio, threw another punch. Hench deflected it with one arm and punched with the other, but he didn't aim for the face, striking the man in the throat. The man swung again, but after a couple of seconds, he realized he was gasping for air. He lost interest in fighting as panic crossed his face.

The third ranch hand charged. Before Hench could react, the man's shoulder struck him in the chest and the man wrapped him up and took him to the ground. The two twisted and bucked, but neither could dislodge the other or get the upper hand, which was bad for Hench if either of the man's two friends joined in.

He pulled the young man even closer, squeezing him in a bear hug. "Hope you ain't fond of your ear."

"Huh?"

Hench sank his teeth into the man's right earlobe.

"Son of a bitch!"

The ranger spit the earlobe into the man's face along with a spray of blood. The ranch hand's grip relaxed enough for Hench to push himself away and rise to his knees. Three punches to the man's face and the fight was over. The ranch hand was still conscious but was in too much pain from his ear, broken nose, and probably some loose teeth to keep fighting.

Hench looked back at the other two young men. The one he'd hit in the throat was looking better, but he didn't look like a threat anymore. The first ranch hand, however, was in a world of hurt. Gabriela kept beating his face, which was slick with blood as were her hands.

"Whoa, Gabby, don't kill the cretin!"

She stopped and looked over at Hench. "He grabbed my tit."

Hench paused for a second. "Okay, couple more."

She made the hits count. The man was barely conscious. Gabriela rose to a crouch and pulled his shirt out from his pants, wiping her hands on it. Then she turned to help Rogelio to his feet. Her husband was still a bit shaky from the punch he'd taken.

Hench went to the man he'd struck in the throat. The man honked like a goose as he tried to get air in and out. He flinched away from Hench who grabbed him by the front of his shirt and hauled him in close. "Get your friends and get the hell outta here."

The ranch hand nodded and tried to pull away, but Hench kept one hand on him and wouldn't let go. He dug out his silver badge from the front pocket of his wool pants. The badge was stamped with COLORADO RANGER. "None of you are welcome back here. Ever."

Hench released him with a shove. The ranch hand stumbled to his friend whose ear was missing a piece and helped him to his feet. The ranger watched them, hand resting on one of his black Schofield revolvers, as they grabbed the man who'd started it all and dragged him from the saloon.

Rogelio rubbed the welt on his face and said, "What took you so long to show your badge?"

The ranger shrugged. "I was bored."

He turned and headed back to his table to finish his dinner of green chili, tortillas, and rye whisky. His knees creaked as he sat, which had nothing to do with the fight. At his age, they always creaked. He stretched his back and got a few satisfying pops, then he smoothed out the front of his faded blue side-button shirt.

Gabriela appeared with another clay bowl of green chili and another stack of fresh tortillas. There was a stove at the back of the saloon where she tended the chili and made fresh tortillas throughout the day. "Gracias, Mr. Hench."

He shrugged. "You're welcome."

"And here's some fresh chili." She started to pick up the first bowl, but Hench stopped her.

"I'll finish that one, too."

She smiled as she walked away. He picked up the bottle of rye and took a long slug. Rogelio had opened it for him when Hench first arrived only about fifteen minutes earlier. A quarter of the bottle was gone.

The ranger folded up a tortilla and used it as a spoon

to scoop up chunks of pork along with diced green chiles and tomatoes, stuffing it into his mouth. Some of the best green chili he'd ever had. He finished the first bowl and went to work on the second, pausing only long enough to belch. He was hungry after riding the trail all day, stopping for the night in La Junta before continuing on to Lamar in the morning.

The saloon returned to its normal state. Patrons went back to their conversations, mostly discussing the brief explosion of violence. Rogelio talked animatedly behind the bar and showed off the welt.

Finishing the chili and tortillas, Hench stood with a satisfied groan and another belch. He dropped two silver dollars on the table and picked up his hat, once tan but now mottled over the years with sweat and rain and dust. He slid it onto his head and picked up his tan canvas duster from the back of a chair.

Both the duster and the hat were the same worn color approaching that of sun-dried horse dung. He swung the leather saddlebags over his shoulder, draped the long coat over a forearm, and used that hand to pick up his Spencer carbine lever-action rifle from the table. Hench still wore his black leather chaps, having come straight from bedding his horse at the livery stable to Walter's Saloon for dinner and drink. The bed he'd find at the hotel just down the street sounded like heaven.

But that would have to wait. As he reached with his free hand for his bottle of rye, two men rushed into the saloon. Friends of the ranch hands. A black Schofield revolver appeared in Hench's hand, drawn and cocked in the same motion.

CHAPTER TWO

The two men running into the saloon weren't armed and neither looked angry or vengeful. What they looked was excited. Hench uncocked his gun and slid it back into his holster.

The men skidded to a stop by Rogelio who was still behind the bar talking with a customer who was looking at the welt on the saloon owner's cheek. All talk stopped in the place as the two men jabbered over one another in their excitement. The best Hench could figure was that something big had happened in town, and it wasn't good.

Rogelio held up his hands. "Slow down, amigos."

One of the men gulped air and then said, "It's Delilah, over at the Satin Perch. She got herself cut up bad."

"She been killed!" interjected the other.

Exclamations of shock erupted in the saloon. With a sigh, Hench picked up the bottle and took it to the bar, setting it next to Rogelio. "Save this for me."

"Si, amigo."

Hench took out his silver badge and pinned it to his faded blue shirt. The ranger looked at the two men. "You say Delilah was killed?"

"Yessir," said one.

The other said, "You don't know she's killed."

"Sure do. Heard it from Emil. She's dead alright."

More exclamations and a hornet nest of murmurs surrounded Hench as he left the saloon. Nearly everyone followed after him. He led the procession down the street to the brothel.

Hench had been to La Junta, Colorado at least a dozen times. He was friendly with Madam Felicity, who ran the Satin Perch and he'd known Delilah personally, or biblically as the case may be. Who'd want to cut up that girl? She was one of the sweeter doves, only stealing from him once.

A growing stream of townsfolk swirled around him as he approached the front doors. It was a large two-story red brick building several blocks down from Walter's Saloon. A crowd churned out front.

Hench shouldered his way through. The inside wasn't any better as far as being crowded. The parlor, resplendent in different shades of red and gold, was packed. Hench stepped up onto an overstuffed chair of crushed velvet to take in the entire room. He didn't see anything but curious gawkers. Jumping down, he shoved his way to and up the wide staircase opposite the front door.

At the top, like following dozens of compass needles, he went in the direction of everyone's gaze. That led him to one of the two-dozen private rooms in the building. A deputy sheriff stood in the doorway. He looked familiar, but Hench couldn't recall his name. He showed the man his badge and went into the room.

Delilah lay on a bed face up and naked, her pale blue eyes staring at nothing anymore, a body's worth of blood saturating the sheet in a red halo around her dead form. Broken shards of porcelain were next to her on the bed and also on the floor. A man, visibly shaken, blood on him, wearing only underwear—no doubt hastily pulled on—sat in one of two wood chairs in the sparse room.

The bed, and the dove, were on Hench's left, the two chairs were opposite the door near an open window. Several lit oil lamps were perched around the room, no doubt brought in after the body was discovered. A small one-drawer vanity with a mirror over it was across from the bed, another lit oil lamp on the top of the vanity along with a big bloody hunting knife. An intricately painted china wash basin was on the floor beneath the vanity and Hench realized it was the basin's pitcher that was in shards by Delilah.

The man was younger than Hench, maybe in his mid-thirties. Sturdy, with ruddy sun-bleached skin used to being outside all day. Doctor Rousseau sat in the other chair as he attended the man. The doctor was in his forties, his skin pale, his clothes clean and pressed. His dark hair was just turning silver at the temples.

Sheriff Eugene Utley, a tall whip-lean man, stood behind the doc and was talking. Doctor Rousseau was patching up what looked like a pretty good cut on the underwear man's arm. He appeared to have other cuts as well, but with all the blood it was difficult to see what was his and what might have been Delilah's. Hench stepped to the bed and disentangled a sheet from the rest of the covers as best he could with his one free hand and covered up the dove. Blood immediately bloomed through the white cotton.

"What'cha doin' here, Hench?"

He turned to the sheriff, holding up the arm with his duster and carbine. "Just got to town. Was over at Walter's when I heard. This the killer?"

The man looked startled, already shaking his head. Not much of the blood on him could have been his, he was too alert for that much loss of blood.

Utley shrugged. "According to Bertram here, he was with Delilah, *in the throes* so to speak, when Big Pat climbed through the window, corned on drink, and went berserk." Utley pointed to the knife on the vanity. "That's Big Pat's. I have deputies out lookin' for him."

"Why'd he leave his knife behind?"

Utley looked at Bertram. "Well?"

The man shrugged. "I don't know. He hit me from behind with that pitcher when I was, um, atop her. I was dazed after that. He ignored me and attacked the whore. When I snapped out of it and tried to get him off her, he cut me a few times and hit me," he motioned to some bruising on his face, "then someone pounded at the door. He went back out the window."

"Big Pat say anything while he did all this?"

The man shrugged. "I don't remember if he did. I was pretty woozy."

Hench looked at Utley. "Know if Big Pat had some grievance with Delilah?"

14

"Not that I'm aware. Felicity is checkin' on the other girls and seein' that someone gets George over here." George was the town's undertaker. "We'll ask her when she's done."

"Sheriff!" The voice came from outside the window. A face appeared shortly after. It was one of the deputies. "Found Big Pat passed out in an alley down the way. Blood on him."

Utley nodded. "Well, there you go. Drag him to the jail, use a horse if you have to."

Hench had met Big Pat before. Not quite an outlaw but certainly a troublemaker. He was also huge and Hench had little doubt they'd need that horse to drag him to the jail. How'd they get him from the street to one of the cells would be interesting to see.

The deputy disappeared and Hench grabbed an oil lamp and looked out the window. Half-dozen large shipping crates were stacked against the outside wall of the brothel. Leaning out farther he saw the name of a tool wholesaler burned into the sides. They must have come from the hardware and feed store next door. There was blood on the crates, giving some credence to Bertram's story.

"Terrance! What the hell are you doing here?"

Hench turned toward Madam Felicity. There were only a few people who got away with calling him by his given name. "Passin' through and heard the news."

The woman glanced at the bed, her eyes brimming with tears. "I'm going to castrate Big Pat before I slit his goddamn throat."

"I'll hold him down for you, Felicity," said Hench, setting down the oil lamp.

She was a handsome woman in her early forties by Hench's guess, but he'd never make the mistake to ask. She had unnaturally dark hair pulled and piled up on top of her head. She amply filled out a red satin dress with an improbably tight corset.

"Big Pat have a beef with Delilah?" asked Hench.

The madam frowned. "Not that I'm aware. Big Pat's in here all the time, but despite his horrible disposition, I never had much trouble with him." She pursed her lips for a moment. "To be honest, I don't ever recall Big Pat being with Delilah. He'd seen all the rest of the ladies."

"What about this guy?" Hench hooked a thumb toward the man in the chair. "You know him?"

"Bertram? He's a regular. Comes in couple times a month. Quiet."

Hench looked back at the bloodstained sheet covering the dove. Why would Big Pat want to kill her? And it wasn't just a murder. He'd seen enough bodies to know that the knifing had been done with fury or lust behind it.

"Did she refuse to be with Big Pat? Maybe he felt slighted."

Madam Felicity shook her head. "Wasn't that way. Big Pat always asked for ladies by name, but never Delilah."

"Bert! Bert! Why won't you let me in? Bertram!"

Everyone turned to the door. A woman was trying to push past the deputy.

Madam Felicity whispered, "That would be Bertram's wife."

Sheriff Utley said, "Let her through, Manuel."

Hench whispered, "This should be interesting."

CHAPTER THREE

Becca Richardson rushed past the lowered arm of the deputy to her husband in the chair across the room. Doctor Rousseau had to sit back, holding a bandage above her head as she went to her knees and hugged Bertram.

"You ain't hurt bad, are you?" she asked.

Bertram grimaced as she wrapped her arms around him. "Just a bit."

She pulled back. "Dear Lord, I'm sorry. He'll be okay, Doc, won't he?"

The doctor nodded. "He'll be fine. If you could move back just a bit more, Becca, so I can finish up."

She sat back on the floor and watched.

The doctor frowned at her, looking at her right hand. "Now what'd you do to yourself, girl?"

"Oh, ain't nothin'. Burned it on a loaf pan this mornin'."

"Come by my office tomorrow and let me take a look at it. You have to be the klutziest girl I know."

"Yessir."

Utley whispered to Hench. "Now that's a good woman. My wife would'a been fit to be tied she find me at the Satin Perch—outside'a business."

Hench nodded, thinking of his own wife, dead now nearly twenty years. She'd have let him know her disappointment at him. But he never strayed during their short years together before she died in the winter of '68. He gave their house in Denver to family and rode off. It was the last time he'd had a place he called home.

He didn't like to dwell on such things, so he moved about the room, looking more closely at the bed and the shards of china. He lifted the sheet covering Delilah, looking at the knife wounds.

Why would Big Pat be in such a rage to kill this girl? Lowering the sheet, he walked over to the vanity and opened the drawer. It held some makeup, a metal syringe douche, with a tin of borax to kill sperm, and some laudanum. Nothing out of the ordinary.

"You look done in, Terrance," said Madam Felicity. "Can I put you up for the night? Maybe have one of the girls give you a bath—lord knows you could use one."

That sounded better than good. He nodded. "Obliged."

"Sometimes," said Utley, grinning, "I think it wouldn't be so bad not havin' a wife."

Hench didn't say anything.

Felicity turned toward the doorway. "Juanita!"

A tall dark-haired dove appeared. The Madam nodded toward Hench. Juanita held her hand out to the ranger. He moved across the room and took it.

Hench entered the sheriff's office a little after nine in the morning. Utley looked at him in surprise. Hench was clean head to toe and his beard trimmed. Even his clothes had been dunked in water and soap a couple times.

"You look right smart there, Hench."

"Juanita refused service until I cleaned myself up a might. She took my clothes while I slept. Feels a little strange bein' in stuff so clean."

The sheriff's office was big enough for several men to make themselves comfortable. There were two desks, Utley sitting behind one of them, and a few hardback chairs scattered. Utley was cleaning one of his two Colt Peacemaker revolvers. Six cartridges were lined up in a row on the desk.

Hench approved. Taste varied, and some lawmen he knew kept the chamber under the hammer empty, but he'd come to believe that the sixth bullet could be the difference between lining up bullets on your desk or being lined up for a casket.

"Big Pat in back?"

"Yep. Help yourself." Utley reached behind him to a small wall-mount metal cabinet that was unlocked and pulled out a key ring and tossed it to Hench.

"Can I have his knife?"

Utley opened a drawer in his desk and pulled out the bloodstained knife. Not a Bowie, but about the same size—big and mean. Knife in hand, Hench looked through the keys and picked the most likely culprit and unlocked the heavy reinforced door at the back of the office. Four cells were in back, the heavy bars were anchored into the building's gray stone. Only one cell had an occupant. Big Pat snored loudly. The bed was too small and the man's feet dangled off the end.

It took two tries with keys before he found the one that opened the cell. He stepped inside. Big Pat was six-five and seemed to be almost that wide. He worked at the blacksmith, but he wasn't a smithy. Didn't have the talent for it. Or the brains. But he was good for moving heavy things. His head was mostly bald, but in a strange pattern as if God had decided only certain random spots should be bald or have hair. He slicked the whole mess back as best he could. He was an ugly ugly man. Hench figured Big Pat might be even uglier than himself.

He kicked the metal-framed bed hard. It didn't move beneath the man's immense weight. But Big Pat woke up. Or rather, he opened his eyes. He stared at the ceiling and blinked six or seven times before closing them.

Hench kicked again and yelled, "Pat!"

"What? What?" His booming voice echoed like thunder through a canyon.

"You awake?"

Big Pat blinked at him a few times, then he slurred, "They arrest you, too, Hench?"

Hench held up the knife. "This yours?"

Big Pat's eyes narrowed and he shrugged. Ponderously, he pulled his legs over and sat up. He rubbed at his face. "Looks like mine. Where'd you find it?"

"Stickin' into a little dove at the Satin Perch."

That jarred him awake. "What? Who?"

"Girl named Delilah."

Big Pat's face went white and he began to tremble.

Hench nodded. "Comin' back to you now? Man there said you was pretty drunk and based on how the deputies found you, it sounds true enough."

"What man?"

"He said you snuck into the room, knocked him silly, then made a pincushion out of the dove. Why'd you do it? She steal from you?"

Big Pat started to surge up off the bed. Hench slammed a fist into his face. The giant bellowed and staggered to his feet, towering over Hench, swinging wildly. Blood flowed from his nose down over his chin. Hench ducked the swings and punched him in the crotch three times before Big Pat finally doubled over and crumpled back onto the bed, curled up like a gigantic baby, his hands cradling his oysters. Blood spilled from his face onto the coarse Indian blanket covering his bed.

In a hoarse whisper, Big Pat said, "I didn't do it."

"You have dried blood all over you. Your knife was in the room and it's covered in blood. You're gonna have to do a hell of a lot better than 'I didn't do it.'"

Big Pat tried to look down at himself, Hench assumed looking for the blood.

"Just 'cause you might not remember doin' it don't mean you didn't do it."

Big Pat didn't say anything, just grunted and held his gonads. His face was purplish red and tears mixed with the blood on the blanket.

"Told you, I didn't do it." With a bit of effort, Big Pat rolled over on the bed, putting his back to Hench.

"You're gonna swing for this. Might as well tell me why you done it."

Big Pat didn't move or speak. Hench left the cell, locking it behind him, and went back out front, locking the heavy door at the back of the office.

"You heard?"

Utley nodded, reassembling his Colt. "Ain't the first murderer to say he didn't do it."

The front door of the sheriff's office was flung open. An older man burst in, thin as a rail with wispy white hair. He was dressed in Confederate field grays creased from sitting in a drawer or trunk. He glared at Hench.

"You son of a bitch, heard you was in town."

CHAPTER FOUR

Utley loaded the bullets back into their chambers. "You two know each other?" He placed the gun back on the cleaning cloth on his desk and kept his hand on it, eyeing the old Confederate soldier.

"Yeah," said Hench. "I know Jeffry Donn ever since we took his unit prisoner at the Battle of Glorieta Pass in the New Mexico Territory durin' the war."

Utley frowned. "You was stationed in New Mexico?"

Hench shook his head. "I was a Colorado Ranger back then, too. Snot-nosed and twenty. Was pullin' duty in Denver when the word came down. Rangers and regulars went on a forced march down to New Mexico to meet up with New Mexico volunteers and put a stop to the Rebs' incursions down there."

Jeffry Donn snorted. "'Put a stop?' You was damned lucky to win that battle."

Utley stood and holstered his revolver. "That was before my time in Colorado. What action was happenin'?"

Hench said, "Rebs took Santa Fe and Albuquerque. They was—"

Jeffry Donn spoke over him. "Command had us marchin' north to the Colorado Territory to take whatever gold or silver mines we could. I think they had plans to even send troops to California to use the seaports. Say 'to hell with you' to the damn Yankee blockade. Y'all were nothin' but cheatin'—"

"At the battle, a group of us was sent wide 'round to engage the Rebs' flank. We ended up capturin' their supply lines. Jeffry Donn, here, became our prisoner of war. But after the war this rebellious cur wouldn't leave, settlin' here abouts and causin' me angst."

"You just watch your back, Hench," said Jeffry Donn without any ire. "I'm still plannin' my revenge."

"Took their supplies so they had to retreat?" asked Utley.

"Cheaters!" yelled Jeffry Donn. "We was winnin' the battle. We was whoopin' you!"

Hench nodded. "Furthest West the Rebs ever got. Them not captured was forced all the way back to Texas after a while. I've had to put up with skirmishes with Jeffry Donn now for the past twenty-some years."

"Whooped your asses!"

Utley chuckled and headed for the door.

"Before you go, Utley," said Hench, "was wonderin' where your deputies found Big Pat?"

Utley frowned again. "Why's that?"

Hench shook his head. "Not sure. Just curious I suppose."

Jeffry Donn hooked a thumb toward the jail cells. "Big Pat locked up in back?"

Utley nodded.

"Good," he said, then yelled, "can't wait 'til they hang that devil! I'll be spittin' on his carcass!"

Hench suspected that was the general attitude in town.

Jeffry Donn said in a normal tone. "She was a good girl, that Delilah. You're gonna swing his ass, ain't you, sheriff?"

Utley opened the front door and started out, followed by Hench and Jeffry Donn. He said, "I'd be mighty surprised by any other verdict."

The sheriff led them across the wide dirt street, side-steppin' a fresh mound of green horse dung. "What brings you to town, Jeffry?"

The old man shrugged. "Gettin' supplies. Visitin' friends. Nothin' special."

Hench said, "You don't live in town?"

"Naw. People get on my nerves. Got me a fine little cabin down the Arkansas River a bit."

The sheriff took them a few streets over to an alley. Utley stopped at the entrance. "Deputies said they found him in there somewhere."

Hench stepped into the shade of the alley, the Railyard Saloon on his right and Jim's Haberdashery on the left. He came upon the blood ten feet in. It was dried black in several patches in the dirt. Utley and Jeffry Donn followed behind.

"What are you expectin' to find?" asked the sheriff.

Hench shrugged. "Just piecin' it together in my mind. Still curious as to why Big Pat wanted to kill her."

"Weren't he drunk?" said Jeffry Donn. "That's reason enough for someone as mean as that sonk."

"Maybe," said Hench.

Utley said, "And maybe it was just a matter of time for him to do somethin' this mean. He and the boys he rides with have all spent time locked up for a dozen different things. Two weeks ago, I had three of 'em locked up for a couple'a days for disorderly. Picked a fight with a crew drivin' cattle east. Always somethin' with them. Yep, just a matter of time with him."

"And why's it even matter why?" said the older man.

"He done it, right? Who gives a fig why?"

"You're right." Hench turned and left.

This time he got to finish his bowl of chili without any ranch hands stirring things up. Evening had come to the little town on the eastern plains of Colorado. Walter's Saloon was about as full as it'd been the night before, but the chatter was much louder.

Everyone was talking about last night's murder. First time a dove had been killed in town. But Big Pat was locked away so no one was scared about it. No one was wondering who could have done such a thing and were they out there tonight waiting for someone else? These were all jabbers reasoning out how someone could kill such a pretty little thing—they'd have been only slightly more consternated if it'd been someone's wife or the schoolmarm. The details, however, were quickly turning into drunken tall tales. One tale had Delilah so cut up they had to use a wheelbarrow for her body to get her out of the brothel.

Rogelio and Gabriela didn't look too bad off after

their own excitement the night before. Well, Gabriela didn't, though her hands were swollen and bruised from the beating she'd delivered. Rogelio had a goose egg on his cheek and a black eye nearly swollen shut, but he seemed to stand a little taller.

He'd stood up to the ranch hands who had been much bigger men. Rogelio took the fight to them, even. Nothing to be ashamed about. The two seemed closer because of it. Hench caught them flirting with each other on several occasions like they were newlyweds. He couldn't blame them. Nothing like a good fight to roil up the juices.

He burped his appreciation of the meal, walked over to the bar and dropped down a silver dollar, and walked out into the night with his now half-empty bottle of rye he'd started the night before.

The spring weather had the night cooling off quickly, but not enough for him to get his duster over at the Satin Perch. He looked up and down the street. Several people were trading saloons in the guttered light of oil lamps hanging outside various establishments. Sighing, not sure where he was headed, he started walking slow. Maybe he'd go back to the Satin Perch to bed down for the night—after losing the day he needed to be on the trail for Lamar at dawn.

There was the hum of voices hidden away within saloons and restaurants, accompanied by the bright clatter of a piano or the smooth strumming of a guitar. Crickets joined in with their night songs to one another. A coyote yipped somewhere on the outskirts of town.

The moon was high and bright. He could afford to take a little time to enjoy the evening and finish his bottle on the way. He stopped for a moment in front of a horse trough to look at the moon's reflection. He kicked the side to watch the ripples scatter the bright disk. Then someone hit him hard in the back, felt like they put their shoulder into him.

He pitched forward into the trough. The water was a shock of cold as he was submerged to the bottom. He tried to push himself up, but the attacker lay on top of him, holding him under, even jamming a hand down hard on the back of Hench's head. The air had been knocked from him by the hit and his lungs burned.

CHAPTER FIVE

Hench was wedged into the bottom of the horse trough. It wouldn't take much time to drown, the air already knocked from him. He couldn't move his arms to get a good enough purchase to push himself up. He tried to twist and buck, but that just wedged him in all the tighter and used up what little precious air he had left. His lungs burned like someone had shoved torches down his throat. However, there was mud on the bottom that slicked up his right arm enough to slide it slowly beneath and across his body.

He wanted more than anything to take a breath. Get a little air into his lungs. One quick gulp of the precious invisible stuff. He forced himself to just think about his arm. Keep it moving before the final darkness took him. Get his arm just a little farther. A little more. What little air he had seeped from his nose. Then he felt the handle of his left-side revolver, forced his hand around it.

The burning in his lungs seemed to set his whole body on fire. His head buzzed like it was filled with hornets. He coughed, his face pressed down tight into the mud. Air went out and water came in. He convulsed. But the gun came free of his holster. He slipped his ring finger against the trigger. His convulsions helped turn him slightly. Not enough to raise the gun between his left arm and the trough, so he pressed the barrel against what he hoped was the fleshy part of his bicep and pulled the trigger.

In the small space of the trough under the water the gun sounded much like dynamite exploding inside his head. But then the weight of the man was gone from his back. Hench lurched to his knees, dropping the gun, puking up water, chili, and rye, and pulling out the gun on his right side. He spun and fired at the back of someone disappearing into the darkness. His heaving lungs and stomach wracked his body and the shot didn't come close to the target. The man was gone.

Several folks poked their heads out cautiously and a few minutes later Sheriff Utley, wearing his long johns, holster, and boots, came running up. By that time, Hench had managed to drag himself out of the trough and lay in a swirl of mud. He couldn't stop coughing and he let Utley help him to his hands and knees so his head was at least facing down while he tore up his lungs and throat. Several more minutes and the coughing started to subside.

When he was breathing more than coughing, Utley said, "What the hell?"

Hench, his voice hoarse, explained what happened.

"You didn't see who done it?"

Hench shook his head. "I got a lot of people who wouldn't mind seein' me dead, but the timin' has me figurin' either the ranch hands from last night or one of

Big Pat's gang."

Utley started to help him to his feet, but Hench hissed. "Careful. Got a bullet hole in that arm."

"The man shot you?"

"Shot myself."

Utley didn't respond.

Hench said, unable to get much above a whisper, "Ask if anyone saw who done it."

Utley turned toward the curious onlookers and called out loudly, "Who was it that done this to the ranger? Anyone see him?"

He was met with silence. Hench suspected at least a few of them knew who it was but were being cowards— or maybe they hated Hench as much as the attacker.

Hench turned to the trough and picked up his bottle of rye bobbing on the surface. Some muddy water got into it, but he didn't care and took several big swallows. "Watch your back, Utley. If this *was* Big Pat's gang, they might be lookin' to put us both down so's they can get him outta jail."

The two walked slowly down the street, Hench dripping water, his boots squishing with each step.

"You still leavin' in the mornin'?" asked Utley.

"Hell no."

"Didn't we just clean you up?" asked Madam Felicity, raising a painted eyebrow. "You are quite literally a drowned rat."

Water dripped over the finished dark brown of the floorboards. Hench started to strip.

Madam Felicity stepped closer. "Is that blood?"

"I got shot. But it went through."

"Jesus Christ. Emil!" A few moments later a tall soft man appeared. Hench knew him to work around the brothel where needed. "Go fetch Doctor Rousseau, tell him he needs to sew up a couple of bullets holes."

Emil hurried out the front door.

"And don't you dare get naked in my parlor!"

Hench stopped undressing.

"Juanita!"

The dove from the night before appeared. She looked

at the madam and both women just shook their heads.

Doctor Rousseau pinched the wound shut and pulled thread through the skin in Hench's arm. The ranger grunted but didn't show any other pain. The bullet hadn't exactly gone through his arm, but skirted the outside creating a furrow that required stitching.

The doctor said, "You're lucky it happened like this. If you had fired even an inch farther into your arm you could have shattered the bone."

Hench didn't have anything to say, but if the bullet had wedged into his bone instead of passing through and scaring off his attacker, he'd be lying dead at the bottom of that trough.

He looked up at Madam Felicity and Juanita. "Where does Big Pat's gang like to hang out?"

The madam said, "You think it was one of them?"

"More'n likely. Even if it weren't, no harm askin' 'em a few questions."

The doctor chuckled. "'A few questions?'"

Hench said, "Talkin' and knockin' heads together is

all the same to me."

Juanita said, "One of the men, Señor Gary, told me once he and some friends took over the Winters' casa. He asked if I'd like to come over and help them clean it up."

"Did you?" asked Madam Felicity.

"Of course not. I'm not loco."

"Winters?" asked Hench.

The doctor said, "Old abandoned place maybe a mile out of town. Next to the King Arroyo."

"I'll find it," said Hench, pushing himself up on the bed, tugging at the thread.

"Whoa, there," said the doctor. "Maybe you should get a good night's rest and let this at least start to heal."

"Tie it off, Doc. They tried to kill me once, I ain't hangin' 'round waitin' for 'em to try again."

CHAPTER SIX

Hench retrieved dry clothes from his saddlebags at the Satin Perch. He placed his boots by a hot stove and quickly cleaned his two black Smith & Wesson Schofield Model 3 revolvers. The trough water couldn't have done them any favors.

Ready to leave, his boots were still quite damp, but there was nothing he could do about that—he'd just have to squish for a while. He put on his duster. Spring nights in Colorado got cold out on the Eastern Plains. He then headed to the livery stable on the outskirts of town near the railroad depot.

It wasn't that late, but he still had to wake the boy at

the stables to get Speck, his young gelding Appaloosa. He was a short and hardy horse he'd come by a year earlier when his former horse got too old for the trail. The young horse was cream-colored with reddish-brown spots splashed across his body.

After saddling Speck, he slid his Spencer carbine lever-action rifle into its scabbard and mounted. He headed south out of town. The moon lit the way in polished silver. The land was fairly flat in all directions save for random burrs from a ditch or small ravine. Scrub grass covered it all, greening now with spring rains but it would turn yellow come the summer drought. Dark shadows grew beneath small clumps of trees and shrubs, marking a creek or some other water source in the otherwise arid land. Off to his right some horses neighed back and forth. Another house or ranch.

He turned off at a smaller trail, nothing more than wagon ruts. According to the doctor this would take him to the Winters' house. Another group of trees appeared before him, marking the edge of the King Arroyo. A dim yellow light could be seen ahead. He guided Speck left of the trail and skirted around south of the house. He tied Speck to a tree, took his rifle, and started in the direction where he'd seen the light.

It was an odd-shaped house that loomed in the dark. It looked like a deformed dog lying down, an exaggerated hump for its shoulders. Scanning his surroundings, he didn't see a lookout. Except for the one flickering light, the house looked abandoned.

Someone was here, but it certainly wasn't Big Pat's entire gang. Hench didn't hear any horses, no muffled sounds of voices. He moved toward a side door. Peering in, the moon showed an empty mud room. He turned the handle and pulled gently. It was unlocked.

He set his rifle down against the outside of the house and then pulled off his boots. In moist socks, he picked up the rifle and stepped inside. His socks were quiet over the floorboards, but unfortunately enough of the boards creaked that if anyone was paying attention, they'd now be on alert. But he kept going.

He moved through the house looking for the light he'd seen from the outside. The house was large and sprawling enough that he took a few wrong turns, ending up in rooms, some bare and some with bedrolls. He saw enough bedrolls to feel confident that Big Pat's men were using the place.

He left one such makeshift bedroom and turned down a hall and was finally awarded by a splash of light at the end of it. He moved more slowly. There was always the chance there had been a lookout and he was walking into an ambush.

At the end of the hall, he crouched and looked around the corner. He'd found the lamp. It was sitting on an old wood crate. The room looked empty. Probably a family room back when the Winters lived in the house. To the right was a table and at least a half dozen chairs. He stayed crouched and listened, waiting to hear someone whispering or even just breathing hard. But all he heard were the crickets outside.

Hench rose and stepped into the room. A shadow

moved out of the corner of his eye. He spun, bringing the butt of his rifle up and driving it into someone's gut. Something whistled through the air and thudded into the wall behind the ranger.

The breath huffed out of the man he'd struck in the stomach along with a weak gurgling cry of pain. Hench smashed the butt it into the man's face. He went pinwheeling backwards, crashing into the chairs and a table and falling hard. Hench flipped the carbine around and aimed it at the man while checking the rest of the room. No one else came out of the shadows.

"Stand up easy. You so much as twitch and you'll have a hole in your chest. Let me see your hands."

The man untangled himself from the chairs and stood up. Hench sighed and shook his head. It was one of the ranch hands from Walter's saloon. Made sense that those three boys were in cahoots with Big Pat, way they stirred up trouble. The young man had a three-foot long log in one hand. He was bare-chested and breathing hard. A white dressing was wrapped around his shoulder. There was no holster around his waist.

Hench motioned his rifle toward the man's shoulder. "That a bullet hole? You get that earlier tonight?"

The man didn't say anything, but he looked plenty scared. He should have. It took all Hench's will not to pull the trigger. This must have been the man that dunked him in the trough and nearly killed him.

"You can let go of your pecker now."

The man looked confused for a moment then dropped the log.

"Where's everybody else?"

Again, no answer, but his lips seemed to twitch up in a slight smile. Hench looked around the room again. Still no moving shadows. No sounds of floorboards creaking. Hench walked over to the oil lamp and picked it up, still keeping aim with the carbine in his other hand.

"Okay, show me to your room."

The man looked confused again.

"Move!"

The ranch hand walked to the hall that Hench had

come out of. The man didn't have on boots either. The two padded back down the hallway and stopped outside a door.

"In here," he said.

"Go on."

The man went in followed by the ranger. He lifted the lamp a little and looked around. There were two chairs in the room. One was draped with clothes and the other had a holster hanging from it, the gun lying on the seat of the chair. Hench went to the chair with the clothes and set the lamp on the floor. He felt the pants and the shirt hanging there. They were both damp.

"You're the asshole what tried to drown me."

The man didn't say anything, looking more frightened.

"Get on your shirt and pull on your wet boots. I'm takin' you in." Hench tossed him the shirt hanging on the back of the chair.

The man caught it and put it on. Then he stepped into his boots, pulling and stamping them to get his feet all the way in. He put his hand on the back of the other chair, next to his empty holster. Hench turned his back on the man and stepped toward the doorway.

When he heard the sound of metal against wood, he spun and fired a shot into the man's chest. The young ranch hand looked more shocked than scared. The gun from the chair, now in his hand, fired wide. Hench cocked and levered the rifle and fired again. The man took a few steps back, into the wall, and then slid to the floor, his chest spilling blood, the wall behind him streaked with blood.

Hench left the body where it fell to leave a message for the rest of the gang. He rooted around for a big blanket and spread it out on the floor of an empty room. Then he went through the house gathering everything he could find and piling it onto the blanket. The only guns he found were those of the man he'd killed. But he had their bedrolls and extra provisions.

Outside, he pulled the blanket to the King Arroyo, walking into the middle of the stream and letting the blanket go. Spring runoff was high and fast enough to carry most of it away. He trudged out, managed to get his boots on over his wet socks, and made his way back to Speck.

The horse's ears flicked back and forth, listening to something, his body tense. Coyotes or maybe something bigger. Hench pulled himself into the saddle, keeping his carbine out. They made their way out of the tress and Hench guided Speck wide of the wagon ruts leading to the main trail in case what the horse heard was the return of the rest of the gang. But it wasn't any of those things. After getting back out to the main trail he heard the distant pops of gunfire.

"Jerusalem crickets." He kicked Speck into a full gallop back toward town.

CHAPTER SEVEN

The gunfire continued all the way back to town. It wasn't a constant barrage. Hench pictured Big Pat's gang spread out around the jail taking potshots more than anything. And who would be in the building? This time of night it might just be a single deputy to keep watch over Big Pat. If his gang were smart—he stopped right there. What if they were all as addlepated as Big Pat himself? They might have started the siege without knowing they were only going up against one deputy. Of course, Utley could have been alerted and he had himself and his deputies inside the building defending it.

Speck covered the distance in a couple of minutes,

though it felt to Hench like far too long of time. They rode hard through the outskirts of town and Hench didn't pull up until he was two blocks from the jail. He dismounted, tying up his horse, and jogged up to the main street.

At the street corner, up against the adobe brick wall of a bank, he removed his hat and peered around the corner. It didn't take long to locate where a couple of Big Pat's men were holed up, shooting at the jail. He put his hat back on and cocked the hammer on his carbine—he'd already levered a cartridge into the chamber.

The ranger moved quickly around the corner. Shots echoed down the street from behind the sheriff's office and jailhouse. The building didn't have a back door, but the sheriff certainly wouldn't want anyone coming up to the back wall with dynamite or a team of horses to try and pull the bars free from the windows.

Hench went a half block down and then crouched in a doorway. Across the street and up at the next corner was the shadowy outline of a man lying on the ground beneath a wagon. Hench aimed, but the shot would have had to be a lucky one.

He didn't want to tip his hand until he knew he could take one of them out. He hurried across the street, to the same side that the shooter was on. The ranger stopped in the deep shadows of another doorway looking at the opposite corner that was diagonal from him. He waited there a full minute, but no shots came from that corner. Of course, that didn't mean someone wasn't there.

He left the doorway and moved forward in a crouch. The man beneath the wagon fired another shot with his rifle. Hench glanced at the jail. The lights were out. Was the man shooting at anyone or just wasting bullets? He wouldn't be surprised if they were all just shooting to shoot.

Hench edged closer. He could see the man clearly, spread flat on the ground, rifle at his shoulder. He decided not to shoot him. Instead, he set his rifle against the wall and pulled his knife.

Easing out into the street, he went down on all fours. The shooter stared straight ahead and squeezed off another round then levered his Henry repeating rifle. Down the street another shot echoed between buildings. Hench crawled right up next to the man and tapped him on the hip.

"What is it?" said the man, turning.

His eyes went wide and he started to swing his rifle around. Hench launched himself, driving his left forearm into the man's throat, pinning him back to the ground. Hench slid the knife upward into the man's gut, near the breastbone. The man tried to scream, but Hench had his throat closed off.

He must have hit the heart because the man struggled for just a few moments before going still. Hench then turned him back face down and rearranged the rifle so from a distance it would look like the man was still in position. He lay there next to the dead man, waiting for others of his gang to fire off rounds and reveal their hiding places.

The next closest was about halfway down the block. He'd be difficult to get to—unless. Hench took off own his hat and duster and then peeled of the man's coat. Grabbing the man's hat, the ranger crawled out from under the wagon and put the dead man's hat and coat on. He retrieved his Spencer carbine from against the wall, and then he moved forward.

He now faced the jailhouse, more or less. He couldn't see any movement in it. It would be almost comical if the place turned out to be empty, except for Big Pat sitting in a cell in back, but that didn't explain where Utley and the rest of his deputies were. They would have been out here in the dark picking off Big Pat's men like Hench was doing. No, they must have been in there. Probably keeping a lookout, but otherwise waiting for the men to run out of ammunition or get hungry or just get bored and wander off.

Or waiting for a certain Colorado Ranger to come to their aid. Hench stayed crouched as he went along the front of buildings, more afraid of Utley or one of his deputies taking a shot at him. The man Hench was going after knelt behind a water trough. The ranger stopped right behind him in the shadow of an awning, the man never turning.

Hench whispered, "Hey," his rifle at his side.

The man turned his head and squinted. "Gil?"

"Yeah."

The man looked confused. "What'cha doin' here?"

Before Hench could reply, or shoot him, another man appeared farther up the block running out into the street. Something sparkled in his hands. A lit stick of dynamite. The man ran toward the jail, pulling his arm back to throw. Hench raised his rifle and took aim.

"Whoa, there, Gil, that's Tommy."

Hench fired. Tommy stumbled but kept moving. Within a second, the ranger cocked the hammer, levered the carbine, and fired again. Tommy tumbled to the ground. At the same time, Hench dove to his right, cocking and levering the carbine as the man in front of him spun around and fired. The bullet missed as Hench rolled and then sprawled his body out, landing flat on his stomach, the rifle at his shoulder. He fired and missed as well.

The thing with such close-range gun play was that the man who stayed alive was the man who could calm his nerves enough to cock the gun and aim true. That wasn't nearly so easy to do with jangled nerves, causing problems with coordination. It was the man at the trough who made a fatal mistake, though it wasn't intentional.

His body betrayed him. His nerves took over and as he levered his rifle, his right hand pulled the stock of the gun down, the barrel rising into the air. That meant it would take him time to aim—only a second, but it was more than enough time for Hench to both cock the hammer and lever in another cartridge while keeping the rifle aimed at the man. Hench's bullet hit him in the throat. The ranger cocked the hammer, levered in another round, and fired again, hitting the man in the chest. He was dead before he finished collapsing to the dirt.

As the echo of his second bullet died out, he scrambled forward toward the water trough. He shoved the dead man to the side and hunkered down next to his corpse. He pulled the magazine tube from the butt stock of his carbine and slipped in four rounds to replace the ones he'd fired.

Out in the street, the stick of dynamite went off. Rocks pinged against the building wall behind him. Something wet landed nearby, some piece of Tommy. Hench waited another couple of seconds then rose above the edge of the trough, looking for Big Pat's gang.

There was a chance they had no idea where the shots came from that took down Tommy or that he'd now killed three of the gang. He wondered how many men were left out here. When he'd talked to Juanita about them, she seemed to think there were about ten, but were all of them willing to attack a jail, let alone a sheriff and his deputies?

Then a man jogged toward him from up the street. He had a revolver in his hand and whispered loudly, "John! Hey, John!"

Hench assumed that was the dead man lying next to

him. Hench said, "Yeah?" trying to imitate John's voice.

The man wasn't fooled. He raised his revolver toward the water trough. "Who's there?"

Hench rose to a knee. The man gawked and fired off two rounds before running back the way he came. The ranger fired into the dark twice, then listened. Someone still running. He'd missed. The echoes of a few men cussing made it to his ears, then the sound of horses galloping away.

Now Hench had to decide if all the gang had gotten the word to retreat. Or were they smart enough to try a ruse, sending a few men off, only to return to try and flank him, while leaving others behind to pick him off if he tried to get to the jail?

CHAPTER EIGHT

Hench stayed put at the water trough. He had nowhere to be and was in no hurry to be there. His carbine lay across this lap, cocked and levered. He had no doubt he could out wait Big Pat's gang if that was their play. For all he knew they were long gone, but he saw no point in risking his life to figure that out for sure. And he'd spent many nights hunkered down waiting for some asshole or other to make a slip up. Of course, Hench wasn't expecting the slip up to come from Sheriff Utley.

One of the deputies yelled from the jail, "You still out there?"

Hench grimaced. What kind of question was that? What was Utley playing at?

"We got us a hurt man in here. We're willin' to let Big Pat go if you let us take him to Doc."

Was that true? Then Hench realized it was Utley who was hurt. Unconscious. He'd never let one of his deputies do something so lamebrained if he was awake—he'd certainly never give up a murderer in the bargain. Hench waited for a reply from Big Pat's gang, but none came.

"Okay, I'm comin' out! Don't shoot!"

"Damn." Hench scrambled to his feet and hurried into the shadow of the building. This could turn into something ugly in a couple of seconds. He went farther down the block, in the original direction he'd come from, then turned back around, stepping away from the wall of the building to try and cover the street for the deputy. He had his carbine at his shoulder and aimed down the street, but he kept sneaking looks to the side, in case any of the gang emerged from another street.

The front door of the jail opened about a foot. A white

handkerchief appeared on the end of a metal rod. The deputy waved it. Hench didn't see any movement in the street—or more importantly, in the shadows on the edge of the street.

Then Deputy Manuel eased his head out. "Don't shoot!"

But there were no shots fired. Hench thought the gang was too undisciplined not to try a potshot at the deputy—or at himself. He felt fairly certain by this time that they had left, but he didn't let down his guard. Manuel came out farther, half-flinched as though expecting to be shot any second. Despite the stupidity, the deputy was brave.

Manuel saw Hench for the first time but didn't recognize him in the dead man's coat and hat. "Don't shoot!"

Hench didn't say anything. Manuel pushed the door open farther and Deputy Tyler backed out holding onto the corners of a blanket. The blanket emerged and sure enough, Sheriff Utley was sprawled on it. The third deputy—Jacob, maybe?—appeared on the other end of the blanket. Hench stayed where he was, covering the street. The deputies, probably still not recognizing him, stopped and stared at him.

"Go already!" yelled the ranger.

The deputies hustled down the street toward Doctor Rousseau's office and home. Hench followed at a distance until he saw them get safely to the doctor's door and bang on it. A light came on a moment later and then the doctor appeared. At that time, Hench hurried up to them. Manuel tensed, but then he finally recognized Hench.

"Sheriff Utley's been—"

Hench talked over him. "You two stay here with Utley and keep him and the doctor safe. Manuel, come with me. We're heading back to the jail."

Inside the sheriff's office, Hench lit a match and looked around. There was a disturbing amount of blood on the floor. "How bad is it?"

Manuel shook his head. "Enough to scare us into

giving up Big Pat. They attacked the sheriff at his house. He got away and came here, I'm not sure how. He was shot at least twice. We heard the shots and me and Tyler came running. Jacob was already inside here keeping watch. We didn't know what was going on, but then we were surrounded and stuck in here. I was so scared the sheriff would die on us. So scared."

"Grab blankets and hang 'em over the windows so we can light a lamp."

Manuel went to work. Hench bolted the front door and then went to the metal cabinet and grabbed a set of keys. He unlocked the door to the cells and pushed it open. In the dim moonlight, Big Pat looked up at him. "Sheriff dead yet?"

Hench walked closer to the cell. "Was hopin' one of the bullets might find you in the dark."

"No luck."

"They comin' back?"

Big Pat shrugged. "How would I know? Didn't know they was gonna try to break me out. Now that's some good friends."

"That's four dead friends so far."

"¿Qué?" exclaimed the deputy from the office.

Big Pat grumbled in the dark, "The hell you say."

"Your friends ain't too bright. Got one at the Winters' place—yes, I know about it. Got the other three out front. And however many is left, you'll swing together. I guess that ain't no big deal for you, you can only die once, right?"

A light appeared up front in the office, revealing Big Pat's scowl.

Hench said, "Weren't enough for you to kill Delilah, you had to try to kill Utley, too?"

"Neither one was my fault."

"What, you stuck a knife into Delilah about twenty times by accident?"

Big Pat sat up. "They done that to her? No foolin'?" There was a hitch in his voice.

Hench furrowed his brow. "Quit your play actin'. It was your knife. We have a witness right there in the room."

"Who? Who was with her? Tell me!"

There was no mistaking the hurt and pain in Big Pat's voice. Hench took a step forward. "What the hell ain't you sayin'?"

"Who was it? Who was in the room with her?"

Were his eyes glistening or was that just the way the shadowed light struck them?

"You know who was in that room because you were there." Hench's voice turned cold, almost shouting, "You took that big knife of yours and cut that pretty little girl up so bad that she was nothin' but a bloody lump of raw flesh. Couldn't even tell who it was anymore. They had to shovel her into a wheelbarrow to carry her out. And you know a whore don't deserve no decent burial. Hell, they should'a just scattered her out back the brothel and let the buzzards take her away."

Big Pat lunged up from his bed and slammed into the bars, reaching an arm out to try and grab Hench. The man was sobbing.

In a quiet voice, Hench said, "Who was she to you?"

Big Pat had his face pressed up against the bars, tears streaming from his eyes, his body rocking back and forth.

Hench asked again, "Who was she?"

"She was my sister."

CHAPTER NINE

"Why the hell didn't you say that earlier?" said Hench.

Big Pat said, "Who was there?"

"Goddammit, you could be free right now if you'd just told us."

"Horseshit. Utley'd never let me go."

"How come nobody knows she's your sister?"

"You jokin'? Anything bad happens in this town and I'm the first person Utley visits, usually lockin' me up for grins. How do you think folks would'a treated her if they knew she was my sister? Made her promise never to tell no one."

Hench stared at him for several moments before Big Pat said, "Go to Hell," and returned to his cot, which groaned under his weight. His body still shook from crying.

"They're gonna bury her proper," said the ranger before returning to the office up front.

Deputy Manuel was on his knees trying to clean up the blood. It seemed like as much blood as drained from Delilah.

The deputy asked, "You think the sheriff'll be okay?"

"I'm sure he'll be fine," lied Hench, as his mind turned over what Big Pat had just told him. "I gotta go check on somethin'. Lock the door after me and don't open it for no one but me or the other deputies."

Before he left, he went to Utley's desk and opened a couple of drawers before finding and pulling out Big Pat's knife. He slipped it into his gun belt. Cocking and levering his carbine, he left the office.

He waited outside until the door locked behind him. There was no movement on the street. The locals were afraid to come out, which was smart, and he was confident Big Pat's gang had left. He walked diagonally across the street to the wagon. Bending down, he pulled out his hat and duster and rid himself of the dead man's belongings, tossing them under the wagon.

He headed back to Speck, turning down the street where he'd left the horse. As he approached, the horse neighed and pricked up his ears. Hench heard the footfall as well and he whirled toward it.

"Whoa there, Yank. It's just me."

"What the hell are you doin' skulkin' around here in the dark?"

"Heard the shootin' and come took a look," said Jeffry Donn. Instead of his old field grays like the day before, the old man wore a pair of tan dungarees and a white shirt. "Saw your horse down here so hung 'round 'til you got back. I'm guessin' Big Pat's boys tried to break him out?"

Hench nodded.

Jeffry Donn shook his head. "What a bunch of

numbskulls."

Hench nodded again; he couldn't agree more. "Unfortunately, they shot Utley. He's hurt pretty bad."

"Sweet Jesus. Them fellas didn't like the idea of Big Pat hangin' by his lonesome?"

"Like you said, they're numbskulls. Thing is, I'm not so certain anymore that Big Pat killed the girl."

Jeffry Donn looked at him sharply. "What?"

Hench shrugged. "Got some work to do, yet, but—well, let's just say I got me some doubts now."

"Come on, Hench, Big Pat must'a done it. His knife was in the room!"

"That's part of the work I gotta do. Figure some things out."

Hench went up the stairs of the Satin Perch brothel to the room where Delilah had been killed. He walked in without knocking. The room had been cleaned and was already occupied again.

The man on the bed grunted, "Busy here!"

"Out," said Hench, grabbing the man's clothes off one of the chairs and tossing them into the hall.

The dove, Henrietta, started cursing at the ranger. The man atop her craned his neck and looked with growing anger at Hench. "If you don't leave right—"

Hench grabbed the man by the arm and yanked him off the dove. He stumbled to his feet and took a swing. The ranger evaded it and slugged the man in the face. He looked confused for a second or two and then his knees buckled and his manhood wilted. Hench grabbed him before he keeled over and pushed him out into the hall naked.

"Henrietta, I'll let you get your slip on, but get the hell out. Now."

She stopped cursing and pulled on a white slip with pink flowers and hurried out the door. Hench slammed it shut behind her and looked around the room. The broken china pitcher had been replaced, the new one sitting in the china basin beneath the vanity. The blood had been cleaned off the wood frame of the bed and from the floor. Both had shellacked finishes and there was no blood left to see.

But he noticed several cuts in the headboard. Either made when the killer missed Delilah entirely or perhaps the killer drove the knife in with such violence that the knife tip protruded from her back. Then he noticed other cuts along the edge of the headboard. The killer had lost all control, stabbing and swinging the knife wildly. Most of the cuts in the wood had dried blood in them. Seven of them all total.

He bent closer. Make that eight cuts. One of them had something stuck in it, making it harder to detect.

Madam Felicity stormed into the room. "Goddamn it, Terrance!"

Hench spoke calmly. "Shut the door."

"You can't kick out a customer like that."

He took his knife out and used the tip to dig at the eighth cut. She moved closer and her voice returned to a conversational level and tone. "What the hell are you doing?"

A little wedge of metal popped out of the cut and into Hench's waiting palm. He held it up to Felicity. "Big Pat didn't kill Delilah."

She froze for a moment. "But—are you saying Bertram did it?"

"More'n likely. This is the tip of the knife what killed her." He took Big Pat's knife from his gun belt. "Big Pat's knife ain't broken."

"Holy Mother Mary. And we were ready to hang the poor stupid asshole."

"Oh, he's probably still gonna swing," said Hench, putting Big Pat's knife away and then taking a handkerchief from his pocket. He set the knife tip in the middle, folded it up and stuffed it back in his pocket. "His gang tried to bust him out tonight. Shot Utley pretty good. If the sheriff dies, they'll all swing."

She cocked an eyebrow at Hench. "What made you want to come back here in such a tizzy to search the room again?"

"Did you know that Delilah was Big Pat's sister?"

Felicity just stared at him, too dazed to comment.

"You didn't know?"

She shook her head. "You sure?"

"Can't be entirely sure, but I left Big Pat bawlin' like a baby back at the jail when I described Delilah's death. I knew somethin' was wrong, but I didn't know what, so I told him all the bloody horrible details. Well, I got a reaction, but it sure as hell weren't nothin' I was expectin'."

"That poor stupid asshole."

Hench nodded. "Even I feel almost sorry for the man."

"What are you going to do?"

"Gonna arrest Bertram."

CHAPTER TEN

Hench woke early and went over to Doctor Rousseau's place. Deputy Jacob was there, Tyler had gone home and was going to spell him later.

"How's Utley doin', Doc?" asked Hench.

The physician gave a little shrug. "He's still in danger. Lost a lot of blood, but I got both bullets out. We won't really know for a day or two if he'll pull through."

The deputy said, "Should we keep someone here, y'think?"

Hench said, "Yep. Until we got the gang round up or in the ground, I want someone with Utley all the time. Where does Tyler live? I'm gonna need his help."

"Boarding house couple blocks away. But he's up at the jail. We thought it'd be better to sleep there, just in case."

Hench walked over to the jailhouse. The spring sun shone bright and the crisp morning chill was melting into what looked to be another warm day for La Junta. Townsfolk moved along either side. From what snatched conversation he overheard, everyone was talking about the gunfight the night before.

A few men on horseback rode by and a family wagon loaded with supplies, pulled by ox, lumbered down the wide street. A husband and wife rode on the bench while their three young'uns squirmed among the nooks and crannies of their supplies.

At the sheriff's office and jailhouse, George the undertaker was across the street. His workers were loading a body onto the back of a buckboard, joining two other bodies already there. With the third man in place, the workers covered them with a canvas tarp.

Hench wondered if they'd found all the body parts of

the man who'd tried to throw the dynamite. In the middle of the street, a man with a wheelbarrow full of dirt filled in the crater left behind by the explosion. He was ringed by a half-dozen kids talking excitedly about the hole.

The ranger knocked on the jailhouse door and called out, "It's Hench!"

Manuel unlocked and opened the door, looking tired and wrung out.

"You get any sleep?"

"Not much," said the deputy.

"Where's Tyler, he get any sleep?"

Manuel shrugged and stepped back from the door. Tyler was sitting on the edge of one of two cots thrown up in the office. A third man, in his sixties with an ample gut beneath a white pressed shirt, black vest and black trousers, sat behind the sheriff's desk. He had white hair slicked back with a white beard, but no mustache.

Hench nodded. "Mayor Davis."

"Ah, good, Ranger Hench. I wanted to talk to you

about the situation. With Sheriff Utley out of commission, I was hoping—" he trailed off and raised his bushy white eyebrows.

"I'm stayin' 'til this is over."

The mayor pushed himself to his feet. "Good, good. The deputies are, of course, at your disposal. I'm going to go look in on our sheriff and see how he's getting on."

With the mayor gone, Hench turned toward Tyler. "Let's go, we're goin' to arrest Bertram Richardson."

"What? What for?" asked Manuel.

"I'm convinced Big Pat didn't kill Delilah. That leaves Bertram."

Tyler stood up and stretched, slipping his suspenders up over his shoulders. "Let me take a piss and I'll be ready."

The Richardsons lived in a small cottage a couple blocks to the east of the jail. It couldn't have had more than two or three rooms. There was a small fenced-in yard with a garden strung with chicken wire to keep out a dozen chickens and three goats.

"Go 'round back and make sure he don't make a run for it," said Hench. "And be careful. If he killed her, he might decide another murder ain't nothin'."

Tyler moved off. Hench waited until he saw him in position, then he approached the cottage and knocked. A few moments later, Becca Richardson opened the door. She didn't look like she'd slept much, either.

"Ma'am, I need to see your husband."

"He ain't here."

"Know where he went?"

Her eyes shifted. She was about to lie. Something was wrong. "Headin' over to the Bixby Ranch. He works there. Be back tonight."

She started to shut the door, but Hench pushed it open, sending her scuttling backward a few feet. She said, "What the hell you doin'? Just said he ain't home."

"I'm sure you wouldn't mind me lookin' 'round some." He didn't wait for an answer.

The place was neat and tidy. Only two rooms. The main had a cast iron stove, a table and chairs, a large chest of drawers, and other odds and ends. Bertram obviously wasn't there. Hench ducked his head into the bedroom. A brass-framed bed with an overstuffed comforter on top, a small vanity set up in a corner.

"Where's the Bixby Ranch?" asked Hench, turning toward the woman.

"I want you outta my house."

"Ma'am," said Hench, touching the Colorado Ranger badge on his faded blue shirt. "I'm the law. I ain't leavin' 'til you answer my question."

She stared at him for a few moments then shook her head and shrugged. "I got no idea. Never been there." Then she folded her arms and kept staring.

Hench stepped closer, but not to try and get an answer out of her. He looked at her right hand, no longer bandaged. Her knuckles were swollen and bruised, as if she'd hit something hard. She immediately ducked it under her arm.

"Thought you burned it, ma'am. That's what you said the other night at the brothel."

"Did I? I don't remember."

"Don't remember much, do you?"

"Are you finished?"

He moved past her and went over to a makeshift counter adjacent to the stove. It was little more than a shelf attached to the wall at waist height. There were cooking implements on it. Beneath it were a couple of pots and pans. To the right was a block of wood with the handles of five knives sticking out. Hench took out one of the knives. A small carving knife. He put it back and then ran his fingertip over an empty slot.

"Mind me askin' where the sixth knife is?"

"I don't remember."

He looked around the counter and poked through several hanging shelves of smaller kitchen items. He crouched down and pulled out the pots and pans. Standing, he went to the back door, opened it, and stepped out into the yard. If you wanted to get rid of a knife you wouldn't hide it in the house. He turned slowly and stopped when he saw a mound of trash—a slop pile, probably for the goats. Freshly turned. You'd get the knife out of the house.

"Tyler? Come on over. Find a shovel and dig through that pile. You're lookin' for a carving knife."

"You serious?"

"Get to it."

The deputy sighed and started looking around the yard until he found a spade. He used it to dig through the pile.

"What the hell you doin'?" said Becca, stepping out into the yard.

Hench ignored her. "It'll probably be at the bottom."

Tyler nodded and kept digging to the immense curiosity of the three goats who kept trying to get in the way of the spade. Hench casually glanced at Becca. Her eyes were riveted on the pile as if it were the most important thing in the world.

Despite the goats trying to help, Tyler managed to clear off the slop. "Huh," he finally said, having dug past the pile and clearing away a small pit of dirt beneath it.

"Somethin' shiny here."

Hench approached. Something shiny indeed. He picked up an eight-inch-long carving knife. Shaking the dirt loose from it, he pulled out his handkerchief. He set the knife next to the broken tip. Perfect fit.

Hench turned toward Becca. "Where the hell's your husband?"

She didn't say anything, her face drained of color, her body shivering.

"That the knife that killed Delilah?" asked the deputy.

Hench nodded, folding the tip into the handkerchief and putting it back in his pocket. He slid the knife into his gun belt next to Big Pat's. He was getting quite a collection. He went back into the Richardson's house and found a jug of water. He poured some into a metal basin he pulled out from under the counter and washed the dirt from his hands. He turned for a towel, there was one thrown on the kitchen table. Becca probably threw it there on her way to answer the door when Hench knocked.

Drying his hands, he noticed a small stack of gray cloth on top of the chest of drawers. A color of gray that looked familiar. He picked up a Confederate tunic and trousers. He looked over for Becca, but she was still outside. He folded them proper and set them back where he'd found them, then he left through the back door, walking past her as she avoided eye contact.

Back at the jailhouse, Manuel unlocked and opened the door for Hench and Tyler. Behind him, the heavy door to the cells was open. A tray of food sat on Utley's desk.

"Marcie brought Big Pat's breakfast. Was just about to take it in when you knocked. Then thought I'd head over—"

"Do either of you know where Jeffry Donn lives?"

"That old guy?" said Tyler, shaking his head.

Manuel nodded.

"Good," said Hench. "You're comin' with me."

"What's going on?"

"I think Bertram might be hidin' out there. Do you

know if Jeffry Donn is close with the Richardson's?"

Tyler said, "Sure. Becca's father and Jeffry Donn were close. When he passed, Jeffry Donn looked after her for a spell. I mean, she was grown by then, but he kinda looked after her. Gave her away at the weddin'."

"Get yourself a rifle, Manuel. Don't know how dangerous Bertram, or Jeffry Donn, might—" Hench stopped talking and looked at the door leading into the cell. There was a rustling sound. "What the hell's he doin' in there?"

Hench looked in. Big Pat's cell was in the far-left corner. The large man leaned his mattress against himself as he hunkered down behind it, away from the back wall of the cell. What the heck? Hench spun around. "Get down!"

The back wall exploded.

CHAPTER ELEVEN

"Hench! Hench!"

The ranger opened his eyes, squinting at bright light. His head thundered in pain. He felt the back of his head. It was wet. Looking at his fingers, they were covered with blood.

"Praise the Lord," said Tyler. "We were afraid you might'a been killed. You must'a taken that chunk of wall to the back of the head."

It hurt to turn his head. There was a fist-sized stone from the back wall lying a few feet away. He said, "What about Big Pat?"

"We got knocked down by the blast. By the time we

got to our feet and in back, Big Pat was through the hole. They shot at us."

Manuel said, "We ran out front, but they took our horses. Then we came back in to see if you were alive."

"How long was I out?"

"Maybe five minutes."

"Help me up," said Hench.

Tyler started for the front door. "I'll go get Doc."

"No. Get a rifle. Both of you, and plenty of ammunition. We're ridin' after 'em."

Manuel and Tyler exchanged glances. Manuel said, "Should you—"

"Get some horses at the livery stables. Move it!"

The deputies left. Hench felt woozy and sick. He stared at the ceiling for several moments before trying to sit up. The room spun hard. He put a hand on Utley's desk to steady himself then slowly pulled himself to his feet, grimacing throughout the process. He waited for the world to calm down. Took a few deep breaths. Wondered if he'd throw up.

"Okay," he said out loud, and pushed off the desk to the front door.

His head still spun but it was calming down. He waited it out and then started back to the Satin Perch where Speck was stabled in the alley. He stopped once to throw up his breakfast, wipe his mouth, and continue on. It was slow going, but he made it to the brothel. He opened the front door and leaned against the doorframe.

"Hello!"

After a few moments a couple of the doves came out from the back of the house. They were probably all in the kitchen eating breakfast.

"Millie, can you go get my rifle and saddlebags from upstairs? Josephine, go get Speck from the stables. Have him saddled."

Josephine said, "You don't look so good, Hench."

"Thanks."

Millie went upstairs and disappeared down the hallway while Josephine returned to the back of the house and out the door from the kitchen and down the alley to the small stables. It was used for the Satin Perch and other businesses on the block. Speck was bed and fed there.

Madam Felicity came out from the back of the brothel. She was in a light sundress. Maybe the first time Hench saw her in anything other than one of her tight satin dresses and corsets.

"You look like shite, Terrance."

"Feel like it, too."

"What's happened?"

"Big Pat escaped, Bertram's disappeared, and I gotta go after 'em."

"Which one?"

"All of 'em."

"Maybe you should rest first." Her eyes narrowed. "Is that blood on your collar?"

"Probably."

Millie came down the stairs, his Spencer carbine in the crook of her arm, his saddlebags slung over a shoulder.

"Want me to put it on your horse?"

"Much obliged," said Hench, thinking he might need to throw up again. He followed behind, forcing himself to walk without a wobble. The sun and slight breeze felt good as they waited another fifteen minutes for Josephine to appear with Speck. Millie holstered his carbine and draped the saddlebags, tying them off to the saddle.

With an inner groan, he pushed himself off from the red brick wall of the Satin Perch and willed himself to get into the saddle. He felt a little better sitting down, though something still tried to break its way out of his skull using a sledgehammer.

He met up with the deputies at the jailhouse. They'd found horses. The three of them rode east out of town, moving at a trot—which did nothing for his head—then angled north toward the Arkansas River. According to Manuel, Jeffry Donn's place was nearly ten miles east. Hench kept a look out for Big Pat's gang. He had no doubt Big Pat overheard them at the jailhouse and was on his way to seek revenge for his sister's murder.

Like most of this part of eastern Colorado, the land was flat, save for a few low rolling hills or little ravines. Hench could see for quite aways, but he didn't see anyone else. The area looked completely desolate, and for the most part it was. Even with the Arkansas River twisting through the land there just wasn't much plant life. Shrubs and grasses grew more densely near the water along with a few trees.

"You two see anything?" asked Hench. He wasn't about to rely on his own eyes, which were a bit fuzzy.

"Nothin'," said Tyler. "Maybe they decided to just keep ridin'. Head for Kansas."

"Don't think so," said the ranger. "Did either of you know Delilah and Big Pat were relations?"

Both deputies looked at Hench in surprise. Manuel said, "Cousins or something?"

"Brother and sister."

Tyler whistled softly. "You think he's goin' after Bertram?"

"Yep."

Manuel said, "Why didn't Big Pat say anything?"

The ranger shrugged.

"But how come neither of 'em ever let on they was brother and sister?" asked Tyler. "Why the secret?"

"When you thought about Delilah, when she was alive, what did you think?"

"Sweet girl," said Tyler.

"And when you think of Big Pat?"

Both deputies said together, "Asshole."

Hench shrugged. "Big Pat appears to have had a tiny noble streak in him and they kept it secret so that his reputation didn't wreck her own."

"Huh," said Manuel.

They rode on in silence. Still no sign of Big Pat and his gang. No large group of men had ridden over the trail anytime recently. That kept Hench hopeful they'd reach Jeffry Donn's place first.

After another hour or so of riding, Manuel pointed. "There it is."

The ranger's eyes were still blurry, but he saw a small

log cabin maybe twenty yards from the Arkansas River. It was nestled in high shrubs and even a couple dozen fir trees. Smoke snaked up through a black round metal chimney. The cabin was up off the ground a couple of feet, built on stilts; Hench assumed to keep it from flooding when the river broke its banks during a big spring runoff.

"Looks like they're home," said Tyler. "Should we rush 'em?"

Hench shook his head. "I don't want us all inside if Big Pat shows up. You two go hide somewhere, a ravine or something, and keep your ears open. If Big Pat shows up, use your smarts. Don't just attack him. Let him and his gang get settled in. Let them feel safe. Then after we've engaged, and their attention is on the cabin, flank 'em."

The two men nodded, and Manuel said to Tyler, "There's a gully a couple hundred yards over here I think. Should be deep enough for the horses."

"Hold up," said Hench, easing himself off Speck,

taking his carbine and slinging his saddlebags over his shoulder. "Take him with you. Don't want him gettin' shot."

Hench watched them ride off, then he made his way to the cabin. When he got close, he could hear the two men talking. The idiots weren't even keeping watch. The front door faced away from the river. Hench went up to it, gritted against the jolt of pain he was going to get in his head, and kicked it in with the flat of a boot. The men gaped at him and the cocked black Schofield revolver in his hand.

It was a one-room cabin. A single small bed was jammed into a corner. A potbelly stove stood to one side. A Dutch oven sat atop it, the smell of stew filling the cabin. A small table was in the middle of the room with two chairs, which sat on a small rug.

Hench shut the door behind him.

"How the hell you know where to look?" said Jeffry Donn after a couple of moments.

"You left your field grays at Bertram's cottage in

town."

"I did?" He looked around the cabin. "Well, dang."

Bertram didn't say anything, just stared at Hench like a child waiting for his punishment.

"You takin' him in?"

"That's the plan," said Hench. "But it ain't that simple. Big Pat escaped. I'm pretty sure he overheard me talkin' about you hidin' out here."

Bertram finally spoke. "To get even 'cause I said Big Pat done it?"

"You picked the absolute worst person in this whole town to pin for the murder. You'd have had better luck claimin' Sheriff Utley did it."

The men looked confused.

"Big Pat was Delilah's brother."

Bertram's jaw dropped and Jeffry Donn looked only slightly less surprised. The old man said, "Well, dang."

"Exactly. Now I didn't see trace of 'em on the trail on the way out here, but he was pretty shook up about his sister's murder. I can only guess they went somewhere first, maybe got supplies, before headin' this way. If we head back to town now we'll be sittin' ducks."

"Shouldn't we run the other way?" said Jeffry Donn. "We're sittin' ducks here, too."

Hench nodded. "True. But at least we're in a defensive position and have good cover. There's extra ammunition in the saddlebags. Jeffry Donn, go on out and let the horses run. No reason to get 'em killed."

As the old man headed outside, Hench said to him, "And don't think I'll hesitate to kill you if you try anythin' stupid."

The old man nodded and went around to the back of the cabin to open the gate of a crude fence. He shooed the horses out of the fence and away from the cabin, then he hurried back inside. He picked up a thick solid board and set it into hooks mounted to either side of the door.

He turned toward them. "There's a plume of dust maybe a mile away. They're ridin' fast."

CHAPTER TWELVE

Hench used the butt stock of his carbine to break the glass out of all the windows. He made sure his Spencer carbine and Schofield revolvers were fully loaded. Jeffry Donn had a Richmond single-shot rifle and a Spiller & Burr five-shot revolver, both from the war—but they looked clean and well-oiled. Hench turned toward Bertram and pulled out a pair of handcuffs from a saddlebag.

Jeffry Donn said, "You can't be serious."

"The man's a murderer. And despite us bein' in dire straits, he might see a situation where he thinks he can plug me in the back and get away from Big Pat."

Bertram didn't say anything. He seemed accepting of his fate since Hench first broke into the cabin. Jeffry Donn, however, wasn't as accepting. "We're gonna need the extra gun, Hench. That's just plain foolish."

"We'll be okay," said Hench. "We ain't alone. Tyler and Manuel are out there waitin' to flank 'em."

"And how many men does Big Pat got?"

"We'll find out soon enough."

He handcuffed Bertram and had him lie on the floor of the cabin to keep him from getting shot. Then he took up a position at the front window while Jeffry Donn set up to Hench's left at a side window.

Jeffry Donn said, "What if they sneak around back? We could use a pair of eyes back there."

"It's early in the day. We got plenty'a sunshine to keep track of 'em all."

Jeffry Donn huffed, but he took his position. Then they waited. All day.

After it became clear that Big Pat wasn't going to attack until sundown, Hench uncuffed Bertram and let him get off the floor.

"Now what we gonna do about the back?" asked Jeffry Donn as dusk descended and crickets started chirping.

Hench shook his head. "Not much choice. I'll give you one of my revolvers and set you up at the back window. So help me, if you shoot me I'm gonna blow your head off. Even if you kill me."

"I ain't gonna shoot you," said Bertram.

It didn't make Hench feel any better. He handed the man one of his Schofield's. Bertram held it awkwardly, making Hench wonder if he'd ever shot a gun before.

"You know you gotta cock it before firing, right?"

The man looked at the revolver for a moment then nodded. On the plus side, however, the ranger's headache was getting a bit better. But when he bent over, even slightly, his head hammered with his heartbeat. Jeffry Donn went to the fireplace and made sure that even the glowing embers were extinguished. They didn't light any lamps so that it would be difficult to see them in the darkness of the cabin.

Just after sundown, the moon rising in the east, they could see Big Pat and his gang moving toward them, taking up positions. Jeffry Donn took careful aim with his Richmond, held his breath, and squeezed the trigger. Less than a second later a man cried out in the darkness. Jeffry Donn grinned.

Hench said, "Good shootin'."

"You was lucky at Glorieta Pass, son."

Hench nodded and turned back to the window. The men had disappeared, now flat on their stomachs. "I counted nine before you shot—not countin' Big Pat, who must be out there somewhere."

"Me, too. Now what?"

"We'll wait until they feel comfortable," said Hench, "then we'll start shootin'. We need them focused on the cabin so the deputies can come up behind and take 'em by surprise."

"What about me?" asked Bertram.

"Don't fire unless you see someone. Your job is to

protect our flank. There ain't much room between the cabin and the river, so if they come 'round back, they're gonna be in close. A shot or two should keep 'em at distance."

It was an hour after sundown when someone in Big Pat's gang fired their first shot. They heard the explosion of the cartridge followed almost instantly by the thud of it into the thick timber of a cabin wall. Another shot and thud followed by a third.

"Sounds like they're comfortable," said Jeffry Donn.

Hench started firing his carbine and Jeffry Donn fired his rifle. The gang out front shot back. It wasn't non-stop shooting, but Hench figured they were keeping the gang's attention. He didn't know how soon Tyler and Manuel would attack. Regardless, he fired slowly so as not to use up his ammunition—the night could be a long one even with the deputies' help.

"I—I think I see somethin' movin' out here," called Bertram.

"Not so loud, son," said Jeffry Donn. "Go ahead and

take a shot. Let 'em know we're watchin' the back."

"Gun won't fire!" he whispered in a voice almost as loud as if he were yelling.

"Cock the hammer back with your thumb for each shot," said Hench.

"Oh, yeah. Sorry." Bertram fired once. There was a pause, at least ten seconds, then he fired five more times. Hench turned to scold him, but Bertram said first, "I got him! I just shot a man. He—he was runnin' at the cabin with a torch. Think he was gonna throw it."

Hench looked over at Jeffry Donn who moved to the back of the cabin and peeked out the window. He turned to Hench. "Sure enough. Someone's down out there and they got a torch next to 'em." He clapped Bertram on the back. "You done good, son."

Bertram held the gun out to the old man. His hand shook.

Jeffry Donn said, "That the first man you shot?" He eased the gun out of Bertram's hand.

Bertram nodded.

Jeffry Donn broke the Schofield open, making sure Bertram watched, dumped the spent shells on the floor, and reloaded with cartridges from Hench's saddlebags. Closing the gun's breech, he handed it back. Bertram still shook.

"Keep your finger off the trigger 'til you're ready to shoot," said Jeffry Donn.

Maybe because of the dark, but Bertram looked extra pale.

Hench turned back to the front window. There was movement. They were staying low, but they were coming closer. At least he had something to aim at other than puffs of smoke in the dark. He hoped his bleary eyesight wouldn't betray him. He fired and a man screamed. The rest of the crawling shapes dropped even lower to the ground.

"They up to somethin'," said Jeffry Donn, having returned to the front. "Where the hell's your deputies?"

"I'd kinda like to know that myself. They seem like good men, can't imagine them runnin'."

The two men took aim with their rifles and fired more shots, but no more obvious hits. Hench could sense Big Pat and his gang crawling closer in the dark. They could be in some real trouble if the deputies didn't show up soon.

"Anything more out back?" asked Hench.

"Nothin' I can see," said Bertram.

Hench then aimed his carbine to his far right. "'Nother torch." But the man lay low in the brush.

"Over here, too," said Jeffry Donn.

Then three more torches lit up the night.

"Can't believe they're this smart," said Hench. "Get ready."

"For what?" asked Bertram.

Neither Hench nor Jeffry Donn answered him as they waited for the attack. It came a few seconds later. Four of the men opened fire, unloading their guns at the cabin. Jeffry Donn and Hench had to duck, but not before Hench saw the man on the far right pick up the torch and sprint forward.

The ranger had to risk it, and he rose up and fired. The man zigzagged erratically and the shot missed. The man flung the torch high into the air at the cabin and then he dropped back to the ground, disappearing into darkness. The torch hit the roof. Jeffry Donn and Hench looked up and waited.

"Didn't roll off," said the old man.

Then, after the gang had time enough to reload, the next barrage started. Another man, to the left, ran forward and heaved a torch at the cabin. Jeffry Donn missed the shot. The torch hit the front of the cabin.

"Well, dang," said Jeffry Donn.

They heard the crackle of dry brush.

CHAPTER THIRTEEN

The brush fire spread in front of the cabin. Hench and Jeffry Donn were more cautious now because of the light coming in through the windows. The old man moved over a few steps and put his hand against the timber of the wall.

"Gettin' hot."

Smoke wafted in under the door.

Bertram said, "We can climb out the back window."

Jeffry Donn said, "There was only five out front with the torches, so there's at least two of 'em on the sides, waitin' for just that. Maybe more now. They shoot you before you could get through the window. We need them damn deputies to show themselves."

Hench looked up. Smoke was coming in through the rafters. The torch on the roof was doing its job.

"We're gonna go up quick," said Jeffry Donn. "This wood ain't nothin' but kindlin'."

"We're gonna burn up?" asked Bertram, looking plenty rattled.

Hench shook his head. "Naw. Smoke'll kill us before then."

Jeffry Donn chuckled and went to the table in the middle of the room. There was a metal pitcher on it. He took out a handkerchief and dunked it inside. It came out dripping. He tied it over his nose and mouth. Hench followed suit, then Bertram.

"Let's see if we can shoot a few snakes in the grass first."

Hench nodded and returned to the window. As soon as he poked his head up, three rifles went off outside, one of the bullets splintering wood in the windowsill. They were lit now, but so were the men outside. He took aim and fired and one of the men bucked like a rat caught in a trap. The other men immediately started to pull back. Jeffry Donn fired from his position. More shots hit the cabin. Hench fired back while Jeffry Donn reloaded.

The smoke from under the door and from the rafters swirled through the cabin. The windows would slow it, but not for long. Hench coughed even with the wet handkerchief covering his nose and mouth. His eyes watered, making it even harder to aim with his already bleary vision. The pounding in his head grew worse.

"Hench!"

He looked at the window to his left, but Jeffry Donn wasn't there. He turned. The old man sat on the edge of a cutout in the floor, a trapdoor open at his side. The table, chairs, and small rug were pushed out of the way.

"Keep 'em busy," said the old man. "And when you come out this way, head west." He disappeared beneath the cabin.

Bertram said, "Shouldn't we follow him? We can get

away!"

"Not yet. Stay at your post. We'll buy him some time."

Bertram looked incredulous. Hench pointed at the back window. "Do it!"

Hench turned back to his own window and started firing. His eyesight was so bad now that there was little chance of hitting anyone. But he kept it up. Big Pat's men fired back in return. Hench called over his shoulder. "Start shootin'."

Bertram complied as the smoke swirled around them. Then Bertram ducked. "They're shootin' back!"

"Keep shootin'!"

Hench reloaded four times, spacing his shots to keep Big Pat's gang interested but not run through all the ammunition. It'd been at least fifteen minutes since Jeffry Donn left. The smoke was much worse.

"I can't take it!" said Bertram, falling to his knees, coughing.

Hench was going to yell at him, but then he had to bend over as he coughed, putting his hands on his knees to anchor himself. He got even woozier by dipping his head like that, the headache hammering away at the inside of his skull. His knees wobbled. He forced himself upright and more shots from outside came in response. A wood splinter struck him in the face. He flinched, but he didn't back away. He fired another seven shots through the window.

As he reloaded, he felt heat from above. Flames roiled inside the rafters. The heat was intense.

Bertram yelled something from the back of the cabin, but the flames were too loud for Hench to hear. The man pointed behind Hench, to his left. Turning, flames were spreading to the inside wall of the cabin.

The ranger backed away from the window and picked up his saddlebags. He stayed low and waved Bertram over. The man scrambled to the cutout in the floor.

Hench yelled over the fury of the fire, "I'll lead! We're going northwest, toward the river. Stay on your toes, no tellin' if Jeffry Donn cleared a path for us or not!"

Bertram nodded and Hench lowered himself through

the cutout to the dirt below. It was cleaner underneath than he would have guessed. Only a few cobwebs and no grass, just dirt. As he bent under the floor, getting himself on all fours, he was shocked at the pain in his head. He didn't think it could hurt that much. He pitched forward, his face plowing into the dirt as his arms gave out. Bertram dropped down behind him.

"You okay?" he asked.

Hench pushed himself up. "C'mon."

He forced himself forward. Light from the raging fire in the cabin lit the space. At the edge of the cabin, they pushed their way through the brush, giving them some cover. He motioned for Bertram to get on his stomach. Here on out they'd be crawling on their bellies.

There was a loud whoosh from behind and fire erupted through the cutout in the floor. They'd gotten out just in time. The roof must have collapsed. There was a distant holler of victory from out front.

Hench pulled out his other Schofield revolver, holding it in his right hand, and kept his carbine in his left, his saddlebags over the same forearm so he could lift it to drag it along. After they'd gotten a dozen yards away from the cabin, Hench looked back.

The front half of the roof was gone, and flames roared twenty feet into the air. He wondered what Big Pat and his gang were thinking right about then? Were they assuming everyone had perished in the fire? Were they letting their guard down?

Bertram tapped him on the back then pointed toward the river. A pair of boots, toes down, could just be seen through the brush. Hench motioned for Bertram to stay where he was. Hench let go of his carbine and saddlebags and slid forward.

They weren't Jeffry Donn's boots. He moved so he'd come in about waist-level on the man. As he got closer, thanks to the huge bonfire behind them, he could clearly see the blood covering the back of the man's coat. Then he saw the dead eyes of the man, his face turned toward Hench. He crawled closer. Jeffry Donn had used a knife on him.

He waved back to Bertram, who galloped past him. The brush behind them was on fire and racing their way. Hench pushed himself up and followed behind. He reached the rocky scrabbled bank of the river, free of brush, before he remembered his saddlebags and carbine. But there was no going back. The fire had already reached that far.

"Damn."

He turned toward Bertram, who crouched right at the edge of the river. Hench's saddlebags were over the man's shoulder, his carbine in one hand, his revolver in the other. Grateful and admittedly surprised, the ranger retrieved his gear, putting the saddlebags over his own shoulder and holstering both Schofields.

"This way."

They went upstream, moving farther from the flames. Hench stopped at a wider clearing where there was a good ten yards of dirt between the river and the brush. The river itself was only twenty or thirty feet across and plenty shallow enough to cross if they had to. With spring runoff, it was faster than usual, but easily passable.

The ranger removed his hat and lay down, dunking his head into the cold water. He left it there for about half a minute, the cold feeling so good, pushing the headache back a bit. Then he lifted his head and drank deeply. Bertram was also drinking.

Hench put his hat back on and rose up into a crouch, raising the carbine. A swirling tornado of flame clutching for the sky marked the cabin. He didn't see anyone through the brush fire, which greedily ate its way in their direction. It wouldn't take long to reach them again.

Hench tapped Bertram and pointed to a stand of four fir trees farther upstream. The grasses up ahead were sparse. The two men, keeping low, made their way there. Hench stood up behind a tree and looked out.

The cabin, what was left of it, burned fiercely, lighting everything in the area. On the far side, south of the fire, Hench saw Big Pat standing there with maybe four men. They were dim shifting phantoms to his eyes—though

Big Pat was a damned big phantom.

He crouched next to Bertram, who sat with his back to a tree, breathing hard, looking worn out. Pretty much how Hench felt. He pulled out a revolver and held it out toward Bertram.

As the man reached for it, Hench slipped a handcuff over the man's left wrist, snapping it shut. During Bertram's confusion, Hench yanked hard, pulling Bertram sideways off balance. He put the other cuff tight around the base of a thick tree branch a couple of feet off the ground. There were enough offshoots along the branch to make it difficult for Bertram to free it.

"What are you doing?" Panic was in Bertram's eyes.

"Can't have you runnin' off and you'll just get both of us killed if you tag along." He held up the revolver until Bertram finally focused on it. "I'm gonna let you have this. I doubt they'll come over here, but I ain't gonna leave you unarmed. And, again, if you shoot me—or try to shoot me—there won't be enough of your head left for your wife to recognize at George's mortuary. Got it?"

"But they're gonna kill me!"

"Then you better hope I get 'em all or drive 'em off. And I'd stop shoutin'. You don't really wanna draw attention to yourself. I'm gonna set this down on the ground. You reach for it before I'm gone and you're dead. Got it?"

Bertram stared wildly at him.

"You gotta answer me, Bertram. You gotta tell me I can trust you with this."

Bertram finally nodded. "Won't pick it up 'til you're gone. You ain't gonna just run off and leave me here, are you?"

"If I don't come back it means I'm dead. So save a bullet to shoot the chain—but only use it if necessary 'cause like I said, you don't wanna draw attention to yourself."

Hench backed out of the fir trees, making sure Bertram didn't grab for the gun. But the man didn't move.

"Don't go nowhere," the ranger said with a wry grin,

and moved off farther west, circling wide of the fire and to get himself around to the front of the cabin.

CHAPTER FOURTEEN

As the ranger moved out into the night, he came across the second man Jeffry Donn killed — knife wounds tearing up the man's gut, one of his eyes gouged out. The man was also partially burned from the brush fire. If Jeffry Donn hadn't killed them, they would have been in good position to pick off Hench and Bertram as they scrambled away from the cabin.

The smoke from the fire was tracking north. The farther Hench moved south, the clearer the air. The cabin fire was dying out by this time, the wood of the cabin consumed, flames replaced with a giant plume of smoke.

He jumped a small ditch with water moving away

from the Arkansas River. That's where he found two more bodies tangled up together. He knelt next to the ditch and pulled up on the top body, revealing Jeffry Donn beneath. To get the old man out of the ditch, Hench had to first pull the top body clear.

Jeffry Donn's knife protruded from the man's side. He returned to the old Confederate. At first, he didn't see any wounds and wondered if he'd drowned beneath his victim, but after pulling him free from the ditch, blood seeped from a wound in his chest. A bullet hole. Whether the bullet or the water killed him, Hench couldn't be sure.

He pulled the old man toward thicker brush, the fire hadn't jumped the ditch, and laid him there. Hopefully Jeffry Donn was out of sight if Big Pat or his gang came looking for their men.

"Thanks, old man," said Hench in way of eulogizing him before moving on.

With the cabin fire mostly out, night pressed forward again. That was good for Hench, letting him move in the open country without being detected. Big Pat and his gang were barely outlined from the mound of glowing embers that used to be the cabin. He eased closer until he could hear them.

Big Pat was speaking. "—leavin' before I know Bertram's dead. We're gonna look through them ashes."

"It's too hot still," said another man. "We'll have to come back in the mornin'. Be easier to see then, too."

Big Pat said, "I guess. I just don't want him sneakin' off free."

"What 'bout the deputies? We can't leave 'em alive, can we? They seen us and all."

"Gotta kill 'em. Dump 'em in the river after."

Big Pat said, "Yeah. After what we done, two more bodies won't matter much I reckon. We can sell their horses over in Lamar. None of us can stay 'round here no more."

"What 'bout the rest of our boys? Shouldn't we go look for 'em? Maybe they're hurt or somethin' and need our help."

"We could split up and—"

"Hell, no, I ain't goin' out there alone. What if that lawman made it out? Naw, we gotta stick together."

Hench moved on swiftly while they discussed the situation. He tried to take a bead on the gully where the deputies had hidden. In the dark, he wasn't as sure about where it was.

When he thought he might be close, he whistled low, so low he could hardly hear it himself. Speck huffed at him. The ranger hurried to the edge of the gully. The moon was sliding toward the horizon in the west, but he could see enough. Manuel and Tyler were hogtied on the ground by the three horses. Hench shuffled down the incline to the bottom.

"You two okay?"

"We been better," said Tyler.

"They got the drop on us," said Manuel.

"You think?" said Hench, taking out his knife. He cut through the ropes. "Where's the gangs' horses?"

The deputies shrugged.

"And your guns?"

"Took 'em with 'em," said Tyler.

The men tried to stand but couldn't.

"I can't feel my feet," said Manuel.

Hench helped Manuel first, dragging him and shoving him up onto his horse. Then he did the same for Tyler. Hench pulled himself up onto Speck.

"What 'bout that old Reb and Bertram?" asked Tyler.

"Jeffry Donn's dead. I'll circle back around after you two are away and pick up Bertram. Now move."

"Can't feel the reins," said Tyler.

"Just don't fall off." Speck climbed the gully deftly. The other two horses followed, and the deputies managed to hold onto the reins. "Head back to town. Go."

The deputies kicked the horses into action. Hench went with them a half mile, then pulled up and waited until he couldn't see the two men and the horses anymore. He and Speck went due north until they reached the Arkansas River, they rode alongside it until

Hench felt they were close enough. He dismounted.

"Stay here," he said, moving off into the dark.

It was a couple hundred yards to the four fir trees. He snuck up quietly, not wanting to get shot by a panicked Bertram. But Bertram was asleep, his left hand dangling in the air by the handcuffs.

Hench went right up to him and took his revolver back and even managed to uncuff the man without waking him. He pressed his hand firmly over Bertram's mouth and pressed his head back against the tree. Bertram's eyes flew open and looked wildly around. Hench didn't move his hand, slapping away Bertram's attempts to grab that hand, until Bertram was fully awake and recognized him.

"We're gonna go get Jeffry Donn, okay?"

Bertram nodded behind Hench's hand. He removed it and stood up, attaching the cuffs to his gun belt and moving off toward where he'd left the old man.

"Be quiet. Big Pat and his boys are still 'round."

Bertram nodded again. The men walked back

through burnt brush. The thick sharp smell of the ash filled Hench's nose, causing his headache to pound again. He held a hand up and showed Bertram the ditch, which was hard to see now that the firelight was gone. The two men jumped it.

Bertram stopped in his tracks, staring at Jeffry Donn's body. "He dead?"

"Help me carry him. We gotta hurry, Big Pat could be right along."

"He was a good—"

"Gotta move!" hissed Hench.

With a bit of tussle and stumble, the two men got Jeffry Donn back to Speck. They draped him over the saddle face down.

"How we all gonna ride that horse?" asked Bertram.

"We ain't. Jeffry Donn gets a ride. We walk."

"But it's ten miles back to town."

"Yep." Hench started walking and Speck followed at his side.

CHAPTER FIFTEEN

They kept off the trail, not that they couldn't be seen by sharp eyes in the dark, but they never heard any riders. Maybe Big Pat and his gang moved on to Lamar after finding the deputies gone. The horizon behind Hench and Bertram turned gray, then pink, then an orange-yellow as the sun broke through the crust of the world. La Junta was just ahead of them by that time.

They stopped at George's first to drop off Jeffry Donn. Hench paid for the casket and burial. Then they walked to the jailhouse. The front door was unlocked and Jacob was inside cleaning debris. The deputy looked almost refreshed. The only one of them who'd gotten any rest lately.

"Tyler and Manuel went home to sleep. We figured Utley was probably safe now."

Hench decided not to disagree with him. "How's he doin'?"

Jacob nodded. "Doc says he should be okay. He even woke up once and talked normal—you know, knew who he was and where he was."

"Good. Any cells in back not got a hole in 'em?"

Jacob nodded. "Tyler said you'd be bringin' Bertram in. Cleaned up one of the front cells. It'll be a might bright and sunny, but it'll hold him. Assumin' the roof don't collapse."

Bertram looked panicked again. "You can't lock me in there if the roof's gonna fall on me!"

Hench said, "I'm more'n willin' to take that chance."

Hench woke up in a feather bed at the Satin Perch. The sun was still up, but his headache was more distant now. Juanita sat at her vanity applying makeup.

"You got blood on my satin pillowcase," said Juanita.

"Gettin' ready for the evenin'?"

"Sí. Though I don't think it's the same evening you think it is."

"You lost me."

"You slept all the way through yesterday and last night."

Hench blinked at her. "I been asleep for over a day?"

"Sí."

"No wonder I gotta piss so bad."

Juanita pointed to the door. "Take it outside!"

"Yes, ma'am."

Hench still felt a bit sluggish, but so much better than the day before. Was that right? Two days before? Wasn't worth thinking about. He headed to the jailhouse. Jacob and Tyler were packing up the front office. Bertram and Manuel weren't there.

"What's goin' on?"

"Hey, Hench," said Tyler. "Movin' over to the mayor's offices. Manuel's over there keepin' an eye on Bertram. We wired the county surveyor. He'll be here in a couple'a days to check out the jailhouse. Told us we should move out as it could fall on our heads. Said we'll probably have to bring the whole buildin' down and rebuild it. Got the Lobato brothers workin' on a temporary place 'til what time we get us a new jailhouse."

Doctor Rousseau entered the sheriff's office. He had a small gash on his forehead and dried blood outlined the right side of his face.

"It's Big Pat. He's taken Sheriff Utley hostage."

"What the tarnation!" yelled Tyler. Both he and Jacob pulled their revolvers as though Big Pat was right outside.

"You okay, Doc?" asked Hench.

The doctor nodded. "He hit me when I wouldn't let him near the sheriff. Then he sent me over here. Some of what he said didn't make any sense. Said there weren't any bones in the ashes. Does that mean anything?"

Hench nodded. "Anything else?"

"When they snuck back to town, one of his men heard

about Bertram being in jail. Big Pat wants a straight trade of Bertram for the sheriff. Says he'll kill the sheriff if he doesn't hear from you within an hour."

"How many men did Big Pat have with him?

"Two that I saw, but I got the feeling there were a few more hiding out somewhere nearby. Couldn't swear to that, however."

"You're probably right."

"You gonna give him Bertram? The man's gonna die one way or other," said Tyler.

Hench pressed his lips together After a moment, he said, "Anyone else gettin' tired of this asshole? Doc, is Utley in any shape to move? Can he walk?"

"He shouldn't."

"Okay, you two go over to the mayor's office and get Bertram ready to move in an hour. Doc, go with 'em and stay safe."

As the men walked away, Hench cocked the hammers back on both of his Schofield revolvers and walked to the doctor's office and house. It was a two-story building with an office and examination rooms on the ground floor and the doctor's residence above.

Hench pounded on the front door. A man opened the door a crack, a revolver in his hand. "Yeah?"

The ranger drew and fired through the door with both guns and then kicked in the door. The man spilled backwards to the ground, writhing and yelling in pain.

Hench kicked him in the head with the flat of his boot. The man went quiet. Hench took the man's guns and tossed them out the front door and followed behind, running around the corner of the building into a side alley.

Utley had been in one of the upstairs guest rooms. Unless Big Pat had moved him, Hench assumed he was still there. But right now, Big Pat and whoever else he had in there, were scrambling in a panic.

He ran down the alley as fast as he could, skidding around the far corner and coming up on the back door, which he kicked in. It led to one of the exam rooms. No one was guarding it. He moved through it out into the hall that went straight up to the front door. Up ahead, a man who was bent over his fallen comrade spun and fired wildly. Hench fired both pistols, re-cocked, and fired again. The man fell.

The ranger ducked back into the exam room and waited by the side of the kicked-in back door. Footsteps ran his way. That would be one of the men who had been "hiding out somewhere nearby."

The man blundered into the room, a double-barrel shotgun in his hands. Hench brought his right fist and the butt of a revolver down hard on his head. The man went to his knees, trying to turn. Hench coiled his body and then uncoiled, whipping his other hand forward from behind his back and smashing the bottom of that fist, along with the butt of that revolver, into the side of the man's face. Teeth and blood flew from the man's mouth and he thudded to the floor of the room.

Hench picked up the dropped shotgun and flung it out the back door, doing the same with the one revolver the man had in his holster. Hench then reloaded his revolvers while keeping an eye on the front door. He didn't expect anyone else through the back as there just couldn't be too many men left in Big Pat's gang.

There'd be at least one more outside who was supposed to be watching the front. Hench had gambled that none of them would be expecting such a swift and direct attack from a single man so soon after the doctor left to give Big Pat's terms. They'd be lax, waiting to get word about when the trade would happen.

Well, Hench was fed up with all of them.

As he finished reloading, Big Pat yelled from the upstairs. "I got Utley up here! Come up unarmed and we'll talk about tradin' for Bertram."

Hench ran down the hall to the front of the building. A man stood in the middle of the street, a rifle in his hands, trying to peer inside to see what was happening. Hench fired both revolvers out the front door, the man dove to the side, and then Hench turned sharply to run up the stairs, taking them two at a time.

The room Utley had been in was down the upstairs

hall at the far end to the left. As he bounded up into the hallway, both guns cocked and leading the way, he turned to see Big Pat standing in the doorway holding Utley up as a shield. He held a gun to the sheriff's head.

The ranger charged straight ahead hoping for the reaction he got. Big Pat let out a yell of shock and instead of pulling the trigger and killing the sheriff, he backed up a step and pointed his gun at Hench, firing a shot. Hench took the bullet in his side and grunted. Utley lashed backward with his elbow, clipping Big Pat in the chin, then the sheriff dropped to the floor.

Hench fired both revolvers.

CHAPTER SIXTEEN

Big Pat wasn't dead, nor was he likely to die from his wounds. The other doctor in town, Doctor Phillips, was patching up Big Pat in another room, Deputies Tyler and Manuel standing over him, guns drawn. Doctor Rousseau worked on Hench. The bullet had gone all the way through below the ribs.

"Ain't this the second time you been shot since gettin' to town?" said Utley, sitting in a chair on the other side of the room. His bandages showed fresh blood from his actions, but he waved off the doctor until Hench got sewn up.

"Shot myself the first time; not sure that counts."

Hench sat on the edge of the examination chair.

"It counts," said Doctor Rousseau, drawing thread through his skin. "Especially since you opened the first wound in your arm and I had to restitch it."

Hench grimaced and drank a big slug of rye from a bottle of Doc's own liquor.

"That should do it," said the doctor, applying a bandage over the front hole in Hench's side. "Switch places with the sheriff."

Hench rose from the examination chair and started to lift his arms up over his head to stretch them out.

"Stop that!" admonished Doctor Rousseau. "Keep your arms down. No fighting, no shooting, no anything for two weeks."

"Can I at least take a piss?"

"No!"

Sheriff Utley smiled and slowly eased himself up out of the chair. The sheriff looked gaunt and done in but better than he had. He walked slowly the few feet to the examination chair and the doctor helped him sit down, then began to remove his bandages.

Hench, helping Utley, walked into the other examination room. Doctor Phillips glanced over his shoulder. He was an older man with a rim of erratic white hair around his bright pink-skinned skull. It looked like his scalp had been spit-shined.

"He wake up?" asked Utley.

Manuel said, "No, not yet."

Big Pat murmured, "I'm awake."

The doctor paused, thread pulled tight through his skin. "Don't this hurt?"

"Like a son of a bitch."

"He gonna pull through?" asked Hench.

"Sure. One bullet went through, and I dug out the other. Were you awake for that?"

Big Pat gave a slight shrug. A tough man—stupid, but tough. Big Pat opened his eyes and looked at Hench and Utley. "Y'all gotta promise that Bertram Richardson hangs for what he done."

Utley started to nod his head, but Hench said, "I don't

think he killed your sister."

Everyone, including the doctor, turned and looked at Hench.

"Horseshit," muttered Big Pat.

Hench shrugged. "I'm just tellin' you what I think. We'll find out soon enough."

"We will?" said Utley.

"Yep."

"It's Bertram, ain't it?" said Becca. "I heard Big Pat took the sheriff. But you sent for me. That mean Big Pat got to Bertram? Is he dead? Tell me!" The woman was in a small office for an assistant of an assistant to the mayor. Her eyes were red from crying, her pale face covered with a sprawl of red splotches.

Utley sat down behind the small desk in the room, easing himself into the chair and grimacing in obvious pain. Hench sat on a corner of the desk. He said, "Your husband's spun us a wild tale, Mrs. Richardson."

She looked confused. "Is he still alive? You gotta tell me—"

Hench nodded. "He's still alive. But he decided to come clean."

"I don't understand."

"Yes, you do. It wasn't Big Pat who killed Delilah. And it wasn't your husband."

"What are you sayin'?"

"It was you."

The red splotches on Becca's face disappeared as her color drained away. She trembled. "What? No!"

Hench nodded. "I've been confused about this ever since the start. First, I couldn't figure out why Big Pat would want to kill Delilah in the first place and then why so violently? Not only that, but he does it in front of a witness that he leaves alive? The man's dumb, but he wouldn't leave a witness. Which begged the question, why was your husband still alive? But then I found out. It was because Big Pat didn't do it. You see, he and Delilah were brother and sister."

Becca gasped.

"Yep. That's been everyone's reaction. And when I

found that out, well, I started lookin' closer at it all. Found a knife tip stuck in Delilah's bed frame. Big Pat's knife wasn't broke. Then you know I found the murder weapon at your cottage."

She looked terrified, her lips trembling.

Utley said, "That's when your husband was suspected."

Hench nodded. "Except that didn't make sense either. Your husband was a regular at the Satin Perch. You probably knew that, didn't you? Or you suspected it, I'd wager. But I had the same problem about your husband. Why would he kill her? And why attack Delilah with such fury and violence? The person that killed her lost control. So when your husband finally admitted that you were the killer—well, it all made sense."

"How can you believe that? He was havin' relations with her in that room. He was there, not me!"

"Wanna know why I believe him? That first night when you showed up at the brothel. Why weren't you more upset? And I don't mean about your husband being injured. But why weren't you angry at your husband for bein' there in the first place? Sheriff even made mention of his own wife and the fit she would'a had. We all took it that you was more concerned over your husband's injuries than his transgressions at the Satin Perch. But it did make me wonder at the time. Were you some kinda saint? But now I understand. When you came back the second time—the first time bein' when you took out all your anger on Delilah—you'd had plenty of time to calm down. Set your emotions straight. But earlier? Well, you butchered that girl.

"How did it start? Were you already suspicious of your husband? Or just curious where he went when he stayed out at night? I'm thinkin' this particular night you followed him and seen him go into the Satin Perch. I bet when you seen him walk in you was crushed. Horrified. Angry." Hench watched her face. Small ticks and tremors moved like insects beneath the surface of her skin, all of them wanting to get out.

"You must have been near mad. I can imagine it. Your

face didn't even look like you. I bet your husband was scared'a you in that moment. Terrified. This wild woman, so obviously off her wagon, your eyes wide and a snarl on your face. I bet you looked like a mad dog right then."

Becca's eyes suddenly glistened with tears and she said in a low voice, "It wasn't like that at all."

"Had to be. You see—"

She shook her head, jostling the tears and spilling them down her face. "I wasn't a wild dog. After he went in there, I walked around the whorehouse, lookin' in the windows. Seen him up in the second floor undressin'. I climbed those crates and saw 'em through the window. Bertram was astraddle that whore, pushin' into her like a ruttin' animal. I was—I was *cold*. I felt like the dead'a winter. I snuck in the window and picked up the china pitcher and smashed it over his head. Like it was nothin'. Wouldn't'a mattered if I'd killed him with it. The girl saw me then, but she didn't see the knife, so she's kinda confused. Kinda angry, until I stabbed her in the stomach. She opened her mouth to scream, but I stabbed her in the throat. She tried to fight back. I stabbed her again and again. I couldn't stop myself, you see. It wasn't until Bertram pulled me off that I stopped. I think if he hadn't done that I might never have stopped."

Hench nodded. "Then I'm guessin' your husband came up with the whole Big Pat thing?"

She looked up at him. "Sort'a. He got me out the window and followed behind me. I wasn't thinkin' of nothin' right then. Everything was, was hazy. I barely remember it, to be honest. Like a dream. I think he just wanted us to get home without no one seein' us and hope for the best. But then we come up on Big Pat passed out in the alley. That's when Bertram got the idea. Had me lay atop the man, to get blood on him. Then he had me hit him in the face a couple'a times—my husband's face that is, not Big Pat's, so it looked like they fought each other." She held up her bruised hand and smiled, a quick quivering thing like a rabbit fleeing before the dogs. "I liked doin' that. Hittin' Bertram."

"Then you went home and cleaned up, your husband took Big Pat's knife and went back to the brothel."

"Close enough."

"Merciful Heaven," breathed Sheriff Utley, shaking his head slowly.

"I can't believe my husband said anything," said Becca.

"He didn't."

Becca looked confused.

Hench shrugged. "It's just the way I figured it played out. But you admittin' it to me and the sheriff? I think that'll be enough for a judge and jury."

About Hench

To get a FREE Hench short story
sign up for the Hench mailing list by going to:

JosephParksAuthor.com

Hench Books

Hench
Blood Hoard
All's Jake
Town of Fear

Made in the USA
Monee, IL
27 June 2022

98706006R00090